FIGHT FOR LOVE

Love, the Series book 3

AUBREÉ PYNN

B. Love Publications

B. LOVE PUBLICATIONS!

Visit bit.ly/readBLP to join our mailing list!

B. Love Publications - where Authors celebrate black men, black women, and black love.

To submit a manuscript for consideration, email your first three chapters to blovepublications@gmail.com with SUBMISSION as the subject.

Let's connect on social media!
Facebook - B. Love Publications
Twitter - @blovepub
Instagram - @blovepublications

INTRODUCTION

To the reader:

Thank you for hanging on until the end. I am determined to make this group go out with a bang. So please know that everything after this page will invoke emotions that could make your thighs clench together and an involuntary grunt escape your lips. If that isn't your cup of tea, you might not want to read this. But baby, if it is...hold on tight, I'm about to take you on a ride.

Love always,
  A.P.

INTERLUDE

Permission [Kwame's Interlude]

You wouldn't believe me if I tell you
Just how long I've been loving you
All these battles I been fighting quietly
These bags I've been unpacking silently
Just to be free enough to cover you
I don't want to be lonely
But I can't be responsible for another
Broken heart leaving holey

Let me touch you
Show that a man's hands
Can mean love
You don't have to be so tough
I've been fighting hard enough
For the both of us.

Just let me unravel your truth
Cut through all that hurt

you've been wrapping yourself up in
Calling it protection
Let me carry some of those burdens
Sitting on your chest

Understand I'm sick of fighting
The distance in my truths
If we're fighting now
It's going to be for love!
Towards us!

Life's rough, but you don't have
To choose to go at it alone.
You could give me your heart
Let me be your home.
Jess Words

PROLOGUE

N adia Garrett
Circa Spring '11

THE MUSIC WAS BLARING and was damn near deafening as Nadia pushed her way through the crowd. She must've stood in line for close to twenty minutes for a drink. Brielle and Wren were on the other side of the building with their dates and enjoying themselves. For the first time, Nadia had let down her guard and accepted an invitation. She knew the minute she agreed to come to this party she would regret it. Outside of the throngs of people in this small house, the cloud of marijuana smoke that floated above her head and the fact that the guy she came with was nowhere to be found, she was happy to be out the dorm for just a little bit.

While pushing her way back through the crowd she spotted Vinny--her date of the evening--posted up on the wall entertaining one of the many girls who'd been trying to get his attention all night. She couldn't be upset that other women found him to be just as attractive as she did. Vinny

Richardson was the star player on the basketball team. Around campus, everyone would refer to the team as Vinny and the Bruins. Vinny was a power forward who had charisma like he had strength. It was a no brainer for Nadia to get caught up in his piercing dimples as he smiled at her and asked her to attend the afterparty with him.

One thing about Nadia; she was always able to keep her mind and heart separate. She knew that there would be nothing after tonight but the same respect she extended to him, she expected to be returned. Vinny apparently didn't the get that message. Looking over the crowd to see if she was looking at him, he shrugged his shoulders and looked back down at the girl in front of his face. With a bite to his lip, he allowed the girl who was dropping bars in his ear to lead him to a room in the back. It wasn't new to Nadia to be attracted or even know men who always got their way. If anything, it was hardening her to do exactly what they did.

Growling lowly to herself, she took the contents in her cup to her head and turned around towards the exit. Her mood had shifted, and she didn't want to ruin Brielle or Wren's night with her attitude. Instead, she would go back to her dorm, shower, and binge watch something on Netflix. It was Vinny's loss for sleeping on her, but he would figure it out when it was too late.

Fighting to get out of the party, she bumped into Kwame. The drunken smile on his face made her roll her eyes and groan in annoyance. He was the last person she wanted to see tonight. "Move out my way."

"Damn, say please or something," he scoffed, stepping out her way. She didn't reply to him. Instead, she folded her arms across her chest and sashayed out of the party.

It could've been the liquor in his system or his will to always win that made him peruse her out the party. "Nadia, why you got to do me like that? I just wanted to know if you wanted to dance with me."

"Kwame," she groaned, turning on her heels. She wasn't expecting him to be so close to her. When she spun around, she damn near stumbled into his chest. His reflexes were faster than hers. Catching her, he smirked and stepped back.

"Come on. It's a party don't be mean tonight," he continued, to just get an inkling of kindness from her. The truth was since he laid his eyes on her, he wanted her. But Nadia was consistent in shooting him down every chance she got.

"First of all, Kwame," she started, "I don't want to dance with you, have a drink with you, I barely want to stand here and talk to you. So, if you would please just leave me the hell alone."

Kwame kissed his teeth and stepped back. "Nadia, you are mean as hell."

"Are you going to tell me something I don't know? Or repeat facts that are known to everyone?" Nadia sassed flipping her hair over her shoulder and ordering him to get away from her with his eyes.

Walking backward from her, he bit his lip and grunted. "One day you're going to be nice to a nigga."

Just as he was going to turn and walk back into the party, he saw her eyes shift from him to Vinny and the girl he was walking out with. He remembered Brielle mentioning earlier that she'd be going to the party with him. It was obvious why she was in a bad mood. Waiting until she started her walk towards the dorm, he shouted Vinny's name and waited for him to turn around.

"Yeah," Vinny turned around to see Kwame walking towards him. "What's good?"

"I thought you came with Nadia?" he asked, furrowing his brow slightly. "That ain't her."

"You know how it goes. If they're not putting out, they got to go. She was being cold to a nigga. I'm Vinny baby." Kwame's lip curled in disgust at his response. Pushing Vinny back with all his strength, he hit him in the eye and watched Vinny fall backward.

"Keep your bum ass away from her," Kwame grunted, fixing his shirt and trailing behind Nadia to make her sure she got back to her dorm. He stayed far away enough so she wouldn't catch him and make his ears bleed again, but close enough to see her. Once she walked into her building, he turned around and went back to enjoy the rest of the party.

His plans were to get drunk enough not to remember what he did. Nadia could curse and gnash at him every chance she got; it didn't change the annoying need he had to protect her.

J une 2017

I

Kwame Franklin

ISABELLA WORKED the room of her newest restaurant and smiled over the crowd. She greeted guest, waited tables, and posed for pictures while Nadia sat at the bar with a drink in her hand enjoying the happiness coursing through the room. Kwame stood on the far side of the bar and watched both women while enjoying his food. Izzy's expression mirrored Kwame's and Nadia's. The road to get this restaurant up and going hadn't been an easy one at all. Financial setbacks due to Kwame's frivolous spending that caused fights between him and Nadia and other unexpected delays, were finally in the rearview. Tomorrow would kickstart a well-needed break for both of them.

Taking the final bite of his food, Kwame inched his way through the crowd down to the end of the bar where Nadia sat peacefully. She hadn't been bothered by anyone all night and she was hoping that it would continue. Nadia could smell Kwame before she saw him. Not because his cologne was loud and obnoxious as he was but because subconsciously, she could sense him. Before he got close enough to her he smirked softly, admiring how her warm caramel leg poked through the split of the knee-length dress she wore. He admired the view a lot more when she strutted in past him. Her scent, like his, greeted him before she could even get close to him.

Kwame had spent the better part of the night watching her from behind his glass. He did a bit of networking, ate here and there but his main source of pleasure from the night was watching Nadia ignore his presence and do what she did best; work the room and make sure everything was running smoothly. He found himself being jealous of the yellow dress she wore with the split down the middle.

This was the first event where their friends hadn't shown up. Brielle and Julian were headed on a family vacation and Wren and Roman were enjoying the bliss of being newly engaged. Their presence was missed but it made them keep focus on the event. Kwame was hoping to leave as early as he could. Although he was admiring her from afar, they wouldn't exchange pleasantries when they were put side-by-side. And although Kwame had found feelings for Nadia, it didn't fully keep him from satisfying his needs. He was sure that whatever he was feeling for her, would soon fizzle and die out because she wasn't going to give the thought a shot.

"You look nice," he greeted, finally approaching her. Nadia placed her drink down at the bar and gave him a onceover before smirking. She was relaxed with knowing tomorrow she would be in a villa on the beach and relaxing. She was willing to be nice tonight for the sake of her peace for the rest of the week.

"Thank you." She spun around in the stool to see Isabella being nudged towards the stage where the band had been playing soft music all night. "You look well."

"I hope you don't have any big plans tomorrow. I'm going out of town and there's a meeting I need you to take," Kwame announced, pulling his eyes off of her and toward the stage that Isabella now occupied.

Nadia looked over at Kwame and blinked her eyes a couple of times, trying to figure out who he thought he was making plans for. "Excuse me?"

For the sake of saving face and not causing a scene because Kwame had her fucked up twelve different ways, she let a smile cross her face. It was painful at best, but she fought to keep it on her face.

"I need you to take a meeting tomorrow. I won't be here it's at three," he shrugged, like it was no biggie, but Nadia was about to let him know that his plans and failureto prepare had nothing to do with her plans.

"Being that I don't work for you and I'm sure that it has nothing to do with Isabella's business, you are on--"

"It's with the property owners of the next location. One of us has to be there," Kwame connoted but Nadia wasn't going to give in at all. She wasn't going to back down. She couldn't remember that last time she had time for herself and Kwame was not going to mess up her time away in

8 FIGHT FOR LOVE

Catalina. "I got a fine piece of ass coming with me on a getaway and being that you have...well nobody, I figured you could take care of it. Throw me an assist."

"You," Nadia smirked, licking her lips before she jumped off of the stool and looked up at him. "You have the nerve. What makes you think I'm going to fold and agree to this bullshit meeting you sprung on me. It wasn't on any calendar and we share three."

"Don't make a scene," he smirked down at her, hearing Isabella begin her speech. Kwame placed his hand on the small of her back causing her to seize up and freeze. "People are watching us."

Nadia positioned herself by his side and removed his hand off of her body. "I don't give a fuck about any of these people watching us," she grunted low enough for only him to hear.

Kwame grinned before pulling her closer and leaning down to her ear. "Don't be an asshole. Take the meeting."

"I just want to take a moment and thank Kwame Franklin and Nadia Garrett for seeing my vision and helping make it become reality. All the late nights, early mornings and everything in between, you two are amazing, I love you."

Nadia smiled at Isabella before pulling Kwame's blazer and pulling him closer. "You have enough pussy to last you a lifetime. You will be okay if you miss a day of being a whore. Take your meetings because I will not."

Stepping out of his control, she smiled and began to clap her hands along with the rest of the crowd. Seeing Isabella wave both of them up on stage, Nadia strutted away from Kwame. Nadia's smile of satisfaction spread wider across her face the further she walked away from him.

Kwame couldn't help but grunt, loosen his tie, and clear

his throat as he headed to the stage behind her. As usual, she had her way with irritating the hell out of him. He didn't know whether he wanted to knock her head off her shoulders or kiss her. It was aggravating and could only worsen the more he was in her presence. He couldn't wait to get to Catalina to get away from her.

Stepping on the stage, he smiled over the crowd and waved before Isabella handed him the mic and urged the two of them to stand side-by-side. Kwame was going to aggravate her as much as she'd aggravated him. Snaking his arm around her waist, he smirked before she fished her hand under his blazer and pinched his side. Chuckling the pain away, Kwame was going to save face.

"Nadia and I just want to thank Isabella for trusting us with her dream. We also thank you all from being a huge part of her success. Eat, drink, and enjoy your night!" Kwame smiled, letting Nadia go. She let go of his side and walked away to hug Isabella.

As Nadia helped herself off the stage, Kwame winced at the pain of the pinch. "Are you ready for your vacation?" Isabella asked, releasing him from a hug.

"I was born ready. Thank you again, you didn't have to do that."

"Oh, I did. I'll see you when you get back."

2

Nadia Garrett

NADIA SAT in the middle of her floor with a bottle of wine that sat next to her glass and pile of clothes surrounding her. As much as she wanted to spend the next three days in Catalina naked, she didn't want to be kicked off the island for her nudity. Her hair was pulled up into a messy bun, with a tribal printed scarf wrapped around her edges. Her UCLA t-shirt hung off her shoulders and her feet were tucked underneath her butt. She was comfortable, relaxed, and looking forward to the next three days of nothing but wine, amazing food, and ocean views.

Picking up the glass of wine and bringing it to her lips, she heard the front door open and close. She counted down the seconds it would take Wren to get from the front door, search the kitchen for food, warm something up, and climb up the stairs. Smirking softly to herself after starting her timer on her phone, Nadia picked up a few bikinis and threw them in the bottom of the suitcase next to a few cover-ups.

"Okay," Wren walked into Nadia's room holding a bowl of fruit in one hand and a wine glass in another. "You got the candles burning, Jhené playing in the background. This mood is set."

Nadia shook her head, looking down at her phone and stopped the timer. "'One minute and thirty seconds."

"It was a hard decision, too. You had leftover Japanese down there...it wasn't enough for two servings, so I saved it for you," Wren smiled and took a seat on the floor by Nadia and poured herself a glass.

"You are far too kind," Nadia chuckled, folding a pair of pajamas. "I'm happy you decided to come up for air."

"Well, I knew that when you get back, you're going to be full steam ahead again. So why not come and help you situate your life," Wren shared, pulling Nadia's bikini out of the suitcase. "When did you get this?"

"Offline," Nadia shrugged, catching Wren's eyebrow raised. A smile crept across her face and she bit down on her lip. "Why are you looking at me like that?"

"No reason. I'm just shocked that you would wear something like this surrounded by strangers," Wren hummed, analyzing her thong bikini bottom. "Are you sure that it's going to fit. You got a lot of junk back there."

Nadia snatched the bikini bottom from her hands and laughed. "First of all, it's a private pool attached to my villa. Second of all, where else am I going to wear it?"

"Well, I'm happy you're alone because that will have

you coming back pregnant," Wren giggled. Nadia squinted her eyes and looked at Wren oddly. "What?"

"I have a gut feeling that you know something that I don't know and it's unsettling." Nadia continued to fold the clothes and place them in the suitcase. Wren looked nervous and tried to hide it under her smile.

So what that Brielle and Wren both had gone behind her back, and solicited help from Isabella to push her and Kwame together for three days. Wren's worry was that one of them wouldn't make it back from Catalina. She was sure the Kwame's body would be floating out in the Pacific if all hell broke loose while they were away. It was taking every-thing in Wren not to let the cat out the bag. Instead of telling on herself, she gulped down her glass and stuffed her mouth with fruit.

"You are so skeptical of everything? Why can't I be smiling because you're finally taking a break. Especially after working with Kwame for the last few months, I know you need a break from that shit."

Nadia huffed and cut her eyes over at Wren. "I know he's your brother and you love him. But that nigga gets on all the nerves that I have. Even the ones I put in reserve just in case I'm feeling patient enough to deal with it some more. Words cannot express how ready I am not to see him for three days. My phone will be off, I will be on island time. So if y'all are in crisis, please figure it out until I get back."

Wren was laid out on the floor next to the perfectly folded pile of clothes. After letting a huff escape her nostrils, she looked at Nadia's facial expression. Nadia's brows were pinned together. Her forehead wrinkled and she bit her lip uncontrollably. She had all the mannerisms of a woman who was completely smitten and lost in the sauce.

"How does it feel?" Wren asked, still studying her face.

Nadia placed the rest of the clothes in the suitcase and stood to her feet.

Walking into her bathroom, she looked back at Wren laying comfortably on her area rug while looking at the crown molding on the ceiling. "How does what feel?"

"To be the strong one and the one who has it all together?" Wren's voice flowed from the bedroom to the bathroom.

"You think I have it all together?" Nadia asked her, gathering her essentials from around her floating sink. "That's not the case at all."

"It isn't?"

"Not at all," Nadia answered, placing her hairbrush and toiletries into a small bag. "I'm the way I am because of how my life played out. Which naturally makes me want to protect the people I love because I know what it feels like to be looking for someone to save you and no one shows up."

"No one who isn't close to you wouldn't know that. They would think that you're tough and you have that shit on lock. But you're scared, aren't you?" Wren asked, sitting up on her elbows. She watched as Nadia's shoulders hiked and relaxed as she inhaled and exhaled.

Stopping what she was doing, Nadia turned around and looked at Wren. These were conversations they had when they were roommates and out of everyone, Nadia trusted Wren the most because she knew her heart inside and out. Wren never and could never house an ill intention in her bones towards Nadia. Nadia held the same sentiments when it came to Wren, and for Wren, she would bend over backward in order to make sure she was ok.

"I am terrified," Nadia whispered. "What if I never get that love and the protection I give everyone else? I mean, what do I say to myself when I'm forty and I'm looking in the mirror and all the work I've done in my life and there is nothing to show for it. I'm accomplished things that I never thought I would, that I was told that I would never do. I made it out of Oakland and I never looked back. I've worked my ass off, but what's next?"

Wren stood to her feet and shuffled into the bathroom to stoop by Nadia. "Whatever you want is what will be next. I knew deep down underneath that man hating exterior and frigid coating that you wanted love, too."

Nadia smirked lightly at Wren pinching her cheeks and making baby noises. "Look at my baby, all grown up."

"Therapy got me super emotional. It's annoying as fuck," Nadia giggled and wiped her tears from her cheeks. "If I never went, I wouldn't be thinking about shit like this."

"I've told you once and I've told you a million times. Everyone needs someone to love them, maybe even you. So, suck it up buttercup and become one with the idea that you may just end up being held at night and enjoying the rest of your life with someone," Wren smirked, knowing all the details of this weekend. She could only hope that Kwame and Nadia would come out on the other side holding hands and loving life. But hopes were just hopes; even though she was emotional about the way her life was going, she would perk up and get right back on her defense.

"Yada, yada, yada," Nadia rolled her eyes and grinned. "I hate when you come over here and get me in my feelings and make me confess things. Why am I paying for a therapist when I have you?"

"Because, there are some things in your life that are just too heavy to unfold," Wren shared. "Speaking of heaviness, when you get back, we have to start planning Kamaiyah's baby shower."

"How is she doing? It's been like two days since I saw her but that's two days too long."

"You two are thick as thieves," Wren chuckled. "I have to undo everything you teach her."

"You will be lucky if your future sister-in-law turns out like me. Then you will have two of us," Nadia teased, sticking her tongue out.

Wren shook her head and sat on the edge of Nadia's tub. "Listen, one is more than enough for me. She's good though. Graduation is upon us, baby shower, a whole baby. Roman and I are thinking about having her stay with us, so we know that she's going to be okay."

"Her mom is still up and down, huh?"

"As up and down as they come, girl," Wren groaned, holding her head in her hands. "Why did I drink all of that wine?"

"Because you make poor decisions to keep a secret, I will find out very soon. I'm sure of it." Nadia gathered her bags and walked back into her bedroom. "Come get in the bed, girl!"

"You are so good to me," Wren giggled, dragging herself out of the bathroom and into Nadia's bed.

"Someone has to be. And if you think that I'm going to send you home to Roman like this, you are out of your mind. I don't want any issues with him."

"Roman doesn't scare anyone," Wren sassed from under the blanket. "I'm going to sleep, have a good trip. I love you!"

Nadia couldn't help but laugh as she put the remainder of her things in her suitcase. Her Uber was going to arrive in a half hour to take her to San Pedro to catch the ferry to Catalina. After she got dressed, she made sure the Wren was comfortable and left to get some much-needed rest in the sun.

Nadia smiled at the sun beaming across her face as she stood on the patio of the villa Isabella booked for her weekend away. While looking over the railing at the shore a few hundred feet away along with the fire pit between the villa and the beach, her phone chimed interrupting her space gazing. Growling lowly after remembering she forgot to turn her phone off, she pulled out the back pocket of her shorts and looked down at the screen. The number was unsaved, but the message screamed at her.

I will be seeing you around, baby girl. Can't wait for you to get home...D

꧁ 3 ꧂

3

Kwame Franklin

KWAME HAD MANAGED to get out of his last-minute meeting, grab his woman of the weekend, and get to Catalina before the final ferry stopped running. More than anything he wanted food and dessert before he passed out and started his vacation tomorrow. His woman of the weekend had different plans. Since they parked the golf cart, she hadn't been able to keep her hands off of him. Kwame was no stranger to women not being able to get enough of him. He already made a conscious decision to not contact her after this weekend was over.

Jumping at her hands grabbing him through his shorts, he fumbled with the key to the door and chuckled lowly. "Almost," he hummed against her lips. "Almost."

He couldn't get the door open fast enough. Soon as they walked in, she pushed him against the wall and dropped her to her knees. "Damn, you weren't playing, were you?"

"No, I wasn't," she spoke seductively, unzipping his shorts and yanking them down to his ankles along with his Polo boxer briefs. "I just want to give you a taste of what you're in for this weekend."

She stroked him a few times before gracing his swollen rod with the warmth of her mouth, making him grunt and bite his lip lightly. Enjoying his impromptu head in the foyer of the villa, he placed his hand on the back of her head as she made slurping noises. She sucked him like her life was depending on it. It was a gift she had, and she was going to use it to make him fall at her knees.

Kwame was on the edge ad she could feel it. She picked up her pace and steadied him by pressing her hands against his hips. Just as Kwame was about release himself, the patio door slid open.

Nadia's eyes widen after laying her eyes on Kwame and bucket of the weekend. "What the fuck are y'all doing!"

Kwame jumped out of his skin after Nadia's tense voice crashed against his eardrums. He couldn't move fast enough to pull his shorts back up to his waist. Nadia's face twisted as the water from the pool dripped from her hair down to her shoulders. She tightened her towel and scowled at both of them. "Hello! One of you idiots answer me. Why the hell are you in my villa!"

"Kwame who is that?" his guest questioned, standing to her feet and pointing at Nadia. Kwame growled lowly and placed his hands on his hips and looked between the two of them. "Are deaf now?"

"Stop pointing at her, she can fight like Rambo," Kwame

grunted through his teeth as Nadia walked over to the counter and picked up an empty wine bottle.

"Why are you in my villa?" Nadia asked, eyeing the woman Kwame brought with him.

He scoffed and furrowed his brow. "This is my villa."

"Kwame I'm asking you a question...who is that bitch?"

"That bitch?" Nadia questioned, launching the bottle at her. Missing her by a fraction of an inch, Nadia smiled. "Get your ass out of here, hoe!"

"Nadia," Kwame groaned as his guest scurried out the villa. "Was the even necessary?"

"Are you even necessary? Why are you here?" Nadia questioned, holding her towel in place.

Kwame stroked his beard and smirked. "The same reason you're here. Isn't that apparent?"

"Listen, I don't care what's apparent and what isn't. I want you and your whore out of here before I find another bottle to throw and I promise you, I will not miss the next time. Get out!"

"Girl, you better calm your ass down," he warned, pointing his finger at her.

"First of all...Kwame. You are the last nigga I want to see for miles! You standing here is pissing me off to no end. Then you have the nerve to get head in my foyer!" Nadia's irritation with the situation was understandable. Kwame could guarantee if he walked in on her doing the same thing that he would flip his lid, too. His temper would come from another place. He was sure that Nadia's behavior came from a place of being set up and he was sure when they got back to the mainland, everyone was going to feel her wrath.

"Stop looking at me like you're stupid. Do you even know her name?" Nadia asked, snapping him out of his daydream.

"Nadia quit your dramatics," Kwame spoke up as Nadia smirked and grabbed the bottle of vodka off the counter. "Of course, I do...it's Rita...Raina..."

"You're pathetic you know that," Nadia scoffed, pouring a drink.

"I pray one day you'll learn to watch your mouth, or someone is going to do it for you," Kwame warned, looking her over. He pulled his eyes away from her, his dick had already gotten him in enough trouble for one night.

Nadia took the contents of the glass to the head and looked at him with a raised eyebrow. "Learn to watch my mouth you say?"

He could tell by how her eyebrow rose that he was better walking out of the villa without getting escorted out with a bottle. "Look, Nadia..."

"Save it. Get out of my face. Take your little whore bunny and go find somewhere else to have your *sexcapades*. So, I can learn to watch my mouth before someone else ends up missing teeth because they tried to make me do it." Nadia didn't break eye contact with him as she poured another glass.

Kwame growled lowly after staring her down for a few minutes. He realized that this was a fight that he wasn't going to win tonight, so he threw in the flag. Breaking eye contact with her, he kissed his teeth as he turned around and stepped over the glass and walked outside and down the steps. His eyes dragged from the sand-covered walkway to where the woman was standing, fuming.

"You care to explain that? Who was that bitch?" she asked.

"First of all, watch your mouth," he warned, stepping closer to her. She looked at him oddly before raising her brows.

"Is that your girlfriend, Kwame?" she asked, looking at him intently. "Is that why she was so mad? You couldn't tell me you had a girlfriend?"

Stepping to her and attempting to get her to calm down, he was stopped by a slap to the face. The sting of it made him stop in his tracks. Huffing, she threw his suitcase to ground, hopped in the golf cart and drove off.

"Are you serious!" Kwame shouted behind her as she flipped him the birdie. "Damn it!"

4

Kwame Franklin

AFTER A COUPLE of hours of trying to find a hotel, he had no luck. The ferry had stopped running and the only option he had was to go back to the villa and grovel. It was going to kill him; the last thing he wanted to do was to ask Nadia for anything especially after she'd launched a bottle at them. He didn't want to be in her space any more than she wanted to be in his.

It's just for a night, he told himself. It was painful just to say aloud but he would have to suck it for just a night until he could get away from her.

Walking up the sand-covered walkway back to the villa, he sucked in all the air his lungs could hold. After trampling up the stairs, he stood in front of the door going back and forth with himself.

"Nigga you might be better off sleeping on the damn porch or a beach chair. Ain't no way," he muttered, shaking his head and scratching the top of his head. "Tighten up, you been through worse." He used his key to let himself in and eased into the house. "Nadia?"

He waited for her to shout some form of obscenity through the house but there wasn't any sound behind her bedroom door. He inched in further and gently shut the door behind him and placed his black leather duffle bag by the door. Nadia was liable to be standing on the other side of the wall with an empty bottle ready to attack again. Poking his head around the wall, there was no sign of her.

Kwame straightened himself up and looked around the living room. There was a book and a blanket on the couch. Taking the book into his hands, he examined the cover and smirked softly. He held Nadia's favorite book, *For Colored Girls Who Consider Suicide When the Rain is Enuf*. He remembered when she was completely consumed with this book.

Placing her book back down on the cushions, he looked down the hall at the open doors. He concluded that she wasn't there. The glass had been cleaned up and the patio door was open, letting the breeze from the ocean flow in. Kwame walked out to the patio to see Nadia slowly strolling down the shore with her arms wrapped around herself and the wind blowing through her hair. Admiring her from afar, he started up another debate with himself. He could stay there and wait for her to get back and have yet another fight with her, or he could walk down the beach and try to soften her up a bit. His charm always managed to get him whatever he wanted, that was until his charm met Nadia. No charm, silk words, or pierced-dimpled smile formed against Nadia would prosper. He didn't have any energy in him to fight with her for the rest of the night. Against his pride, he found himself traveling down to the beach.

Trailing in her footsteps, he decided to get closer before calling her name. He would have to shout over the waves crashing and the wind. Finally, reaching her, he reached out and touched her elbow. Nadia spun around ready to knock his head off his shoulders. "WHAT IS WRONG WITH YOU!" She was startled, and it took a moment for her to catch her breath and look him over. "Don't do that. I almost punched the hell out of you. Not that you wouldn't deserve it."

Kwame sighed and looked away from her at the water that danced under the moonlight. "I thought I kicked you out?"

"You did and I'm back." He shrugged his shoulders, looking back her and the grimace that took over her face. "Every hotel on the island is booked."

"And what does that have to do with me? Nothing," she scoffed and turned to walk away. On impulse, he reached out and pulled her back. "What have I told you about touching me."

Kwame threw his hands up in the air and looked down at his feisty enemy. "Look, it's just for tonight. I promise that in the morning, I will be out of your space. Even though Isabella clearly booked the villa for the both of us."

Rolling her eyes, she crossed her arms over her chest. "As much I don't want to look at you for the next three days, this is what it is. You keep your freak fest away from me and I will not bother you."

Kwame smirked, surprised that Nadia folded so easily. Normally, she would fight back with tooth and nail, but he sensed that something else was on her mind. He nodded as she turned to walk away. He couldn't help himself; he had the need to be by her.

To protect her.

To make sure that while she was in her head, she was in perfect peace.

"What are you doing?" she asked, looking at him stroll alongside her. "Get away from me."

"No," he replied stern enough for her mouth to drop open and her eye twitch. "You shouldn't be walking by yourself anyway. Come on."

Nadia didn't say anything for a couple of minutes before she fixed her mouth to talk. "I do everything alone."

"That's because you're mean as hell."

"I have my reasons," she mumbled, holding herself tighter. Kwame traced his bottom lip with the tip of his tongue and cleared his throat.

"Am I correct to say that guy in Oakland is a part of the reason? What's he? An ex?" Kwame nor any of the guys ever got the details on what happened to her, to make her react the way she did. Kwame realized that Nadia reacted more than she thought the situation out.

Nadia laughed silently. "An ex...no."

She hesitated for a moment on whether or not to tell Kwame who Donte was to her. She didn't want anyone walking around thinking she would actually choose Donte to be with. "He's my rapist."

Attempting to remain strong, she shrugged her shoulders like it was nothing. But the news froze Kwame in his tracks. He felt his heart drop, his mouth fell open, and he felt like an asshole for how much hell he gave her behind it. "When... I mean why..."

He stopped to collect his thoughts and shoved his hands in his pocket and sighed. "I mean, I'm sorry. I didn't know."

"Nobody did until that night. I'm normally very good at keeping my shit to myself. It keeps people from pitying me."

"It's not about pity, it's about telling the people around you so they can help you carry that. I don't know what I would do if Wren told me some shit like that."

Nadia watched the water rush across her feet then descend. "That's why I'm the way I am. I mean, granted; I don't like you. But I'm extra guarded because I remember how it was to have nobody to protect me. Even now, I'm the one doing most of the protecting. I wanted protection; I didn't have it, so I became what I needed."

If you only knew.

"Where were your parents?" Kwame wanted to know every detail. That need he had to protect her was taking over his being. If he knew, he would try to take that away from her. Somehow, someway.

"Mom was at work. Dad was gambling the rent money away. She would leave me with the lady down the block, who had a son who didn't know how to keep his hands to himself." Nadia bit her lip and shrugged her shoulders. "Long story short, I ended up pregnant and lost it. No biggie. I'm in therapy twice a week."

"Damn," he whistled, feeling an ache in his heart. "That shit is heavy."

"It is what it is, you know. Shit happens. I'm just trying to get myself right and keep moving on with my life."

"Will you ever go back?"

Nadia looked up and him and smirked a little. "You're full of questions, huh?"

Kwame let a nervous laugh escape his being. Around Nadia, he had no need to be cool he just wanted to be in her space. This was the first time in years where they were trading insults like Kyle and Max from *Living Single.* "You don't talk to me unless you're barking some demand at me, telling me I'm a hoe, a dog. Threatening me or whatever else it is that you do."

"You are a whore, Kwame. You should accept that fact. You were just getting head in the foyer an hour and a half ago. That in itself is enough evidence to support my reasoning. Let's not mention the years of documentation I have on the women you kept for a day or two. You were actually going to keep her around for three days?" Nadia was amused with the thought of him being able to be in the same space with a woman for three days and he didn't even know her name.

"I'm not. I'm just a man with needs," he shared, causing Nadia to groan and curl her lip upward.

"I am not doing this with you. You should accept the fact that you are what you are. By the time you settle down you're going to be old and tired."

"If I settle down," he admitted. "My options of life partners are low."

Nadia burst out in laughter, stopping in her tracks. "Please stop it."

Her laughter was contagious. "What is so damn funny?"

"You are funny." Nadia wiped a tear from her eye. "My options of life partners are low."

"That's funny? That I need a good woman to share my life with and I'm surrounded by fast ass, money grabbing women?"

"Kwame," Nadia finally settled her laughing and sighed. "You are fast and money grabbing. You attract exactly what you are."

"And what do you attract?" he fired back, looking back at her. The moon shined on her face that still held a smile. Nadia shrugged her shoulders.

"Nothing because I've chosen not to have anyone to share my life with," she hummed before turning around and walking back to the villa. As she turned around, he caught a glimpse of her smile dropping and a lone tear.

Running his hand over his waves, he sighed and looked at the water. She was well within his vantage point, so he let her walk alone as he slowly trailed behind her. "Shit."

Just as quickly as she opened up to him, she shut down. His mission had shifted from crashing for a night to seeing if he could crack her open before they departed. Kwame lingered on the beach until Nadia had disappeared into the house. He walked slowly toward the villa and let their conversation marinate. Like a smitten boy in high school, he smiled wide now that he was by himself. It was uncertain how much longer he could hide his growing feelings for her. His fear, like normal, was that his feelings wouldn't be replicated. Nadia had already voiced her disdain for him. Part of him was willing to accept the defeat and keep his distance from her. But that same part of him would regret it if she ended up with someone else. On the other hand, he wanted to make her want him, so she had no other option but to fall into his arms.

It was hopeless the way he daydreamed about it. Underneath the cool, collected and suave demeanor he idolized love and being in love. He had never been his best self until he was in love. Even though that relationship fell through the cracks and could never be redeemed, he prayed that one day he would have a woman in his life that would make him be a better man.

Finally reaching the villa, he walked lightly through the

sliding door. Locking the door behind him, he shuffled into the kitchen and poured a glass of tequila. Snickering under his breath, he made sure to give Isabella an ear full about this slip-up. Nadia and Kwame would have never had a civil conversation if it hadn't been for Isabella. Leaning on the counter, he looked over Nadia's handwritten itinerary on the counter.

"Full body massage at ten," he grunted before taking the rest of the contents of the glass to the head. "She needs something to loosen her ass up."

Smirking softly to himself, he placed the glass in the sink and shuffled over to the front door to get his duffle bag and head down to the unoccupied guest room.

After taking a shower, Kwame opened the window and let the ocean breeze grace his bare chest. Lying in the bed, he looked up at the ceiling and sighed. "What are you going to do, Kwa?"

Laying still until his body relaxed, his mind was made up. He would need to handle this with finesse moving forward. Soon, the breeze helped drift him off to sleep while his plan formulated in the front of his mind.

5

Kwame Franklin

SOUNDS OF CHILDREN laughing from the beach woke him out of his sleep. Reluctantly sitting up, he looked around the room and stretched followed by a wide yawn. He hadn't slept like that in weeks. It could have been the breeze from the ocean or that settling feeling of Nadia being in the other room. Once the sleep was gone from his eyes, he shuffled down the hall past Nadia's room and into the kitchen. Pulling the door of the fridge open, he smirked at Isabella's ability to never leave a detail unturned. The fridge was packed from top to bottom with everything they would need. Spotting the chocolate syrup, strawberries and whip cream, he couldn't help but shake his head. "She's tripping big time."

Reaching past the novelties, he pulled out the fruit and bread. His plan was to go for a run along the beach, so breakfast would be light. Whatever he made for himself, he would make enough for Nadia when she got up. One thing he knew for sure was that she loved to eat, and she would probably wake up hungry. Cutting up the mangos, pineapples, and strawberries, Kwame put them in a bowl while the bread toasted in the toaster.

Munching on his breakfast, he looked over the list of activities on the brochure on the counter. When he was done, he cleaned up, placed the bowl of fruit on the first shelf of the fridge and two slices of bread in the toaster so Nadia could start it. Kwame grabbed a pen and paper and wrote her a note before walking back down the hall. Pulling his running tights over his legs followed by a pair of shorts, he put his sneakers on and silently slipped out of the patio door.

With his headphones blasting his workout playlist in his ears, he started his run. Last night was still reeling in his mind. He let his mind trail off on why he needed to be validated by picking up women and dropping them like a bad habit. The very thing he emulated about his father was the very thing that broke his mother's heart. He knew that he could talk a woman out of her panties within moments without too much effort at all. They all fell like putty into his hands. He rarely handled them with care and he definitely didn't care about how it felt to be on the receiving end of his abuse.

While his feet were pounding against the sand and his heart pounding against his chest, he tried to figure out why Nadia had such a heavy effect on him. Why was she the one thing that he couldn't get and still managed to drive him crazy? He wondered if this was God's way of making him really slow down to appreciate the view and smell the flowers. To be the man that he wished his mother had while she was spending her days, trying to get over Terry and the mess of her heart he left her with.

I got to get her comfortable.

His mind was racing. Nadia would never give in to him if he didn't make conscious strides to make her feel comfortable and secure. He picked that up from the night before; constantly looking over her shoulder, jumping when he snuck up on her and her need to always protect herself. Once he had her comfortable, he could make her feel secure. The ultimate task would be to make sure that he handled her heart with care, if and when she gave it to him. Until then, he would have to show her a change in order to capture her attention. Nadia was new territory and had to be surveyed carefully before he started his work. By the time they left Catalina, Kwame was going to have everything he needed to break her down and get past her walls, guards, and barriers surrounding her heart.

Nadia Garrett

SHE LAID in bed for an hour without moving. It felt wonderful not to have her phone ring off the hook, and not have people wanting her to answer questions or giving directions on things they could figure out on their own. She was relaxed for the first time in months and didn't have any cares in the world. Sprawled across the bed, she let the breeze from the ocean dance across her body. After a few minutes of laying across the bed with her eyes closed, she opened them and looked around the room and hummed at the serenity. She wanted to cuss Isabella out for the stunt she pulled but she couldn't be as upset as she wanted because this was such a great gift.

Nadia could easily ignore Kwame. She's been doing it for years so what was a few days in his presence. She could use this time away from the noise of L.A. to reflect on the things that her therapist had suggested. Nadia was charged with identifying the things that triggered her and made her want to lash out. The biggest thing that was bothering her now was Donte's reappearance. She'd tried her best to hide how much his energy had disturbed her, but it was becoming almost impossible. When Kwame snuck up on her at the beach, she knew that it was Donte and he'd followed her here. She wasn't sure how much longer she could hide him being in L.A. from everyone. She was so worried about not disturbing anyone else's energy, that she would have to fight three times harder to protect herself from him.

Rolling on her back, she looked up at the ceiling and groaned at the thought. She just wanted him to go as far away from her as possible. There was no need to bring up the past and threaten her. She was trying to move on from everything he'd ever done to hurt her. For years, all she's wanted to do was cause as much pain to anyone that caused pain to her. Anyone who broke her heart, anyone who abandoned her, abused her, lied to her, lied on her, disrespected her; she wanted to rain down hellfire on them. All that was probably the underlying reason why she wouldn't let Kwame too close to her. She had to ward him off. She knew what type of man he was, and he could do damage. If he were to get close enough to hurt her, their group dynamic would never be the same.

Nadia sat up on her arms and toyed with the idea of

lying in the bed all day. As much as she wanted to, she had a massage that she had to get to. She fully sat up in the bed, ran her hands through her hair, pulled her clip-ins out and threw her legs over the edge of the bed. Ejecting herself from the bed, she strutted into the bathroom to get ready for her day. Once the massage was over, she was going to check out a few of the local shops and if she felt up to it, walk around the botanical gardens.

Dressing in a flowy sundress, she pulled her hair into a high bun. She kept her make-up to minimum; she wasn't in the business of trying to impress anyone. She was going to spend the day with herself and she didn't need to look like a model for herself. Nadia spritzed a light mist of Daisy over her bare skin before walking out of her room. Closing the door behind her, she walked into the kitchen to see a note from Kwame on the countertop.

I'm not leaving...but the fruit is in the fridge and bread is in the toaster. Enjoy your spa day.

Rolling her eyes, she pressed her lips together tightly in order not to smile wide as her face wanted. Pulling the door of the fridge open, she pulled a small bowl of fruit off the shelf, closed the door with her hip and pressed the button of the toaster down. The small gesture made her consider being nicer to him, even if it were just for another day and a half.

After she ate, she grabbed her purse, slipped her feet into her sandals and headed to her spa appointment. When she returned to the villa, she wanted to be less tense and calmer.

THE SPA DAY and the shopping were exactly what the

doctor ordered. Walking back into the villa with her bags in hand, she was hit by the smell of something amazing cooking. On her way back, she decided that she was going to shower and go back out for food later. She wasn't expecting to see Kwame in the kitchen cooking. With her eyes squinted in his direction, she watched quietly while he tended to the pots and bopped his head along with the music coming from the speakers. Before she could turn to walk down the hall, he looked over his shoulder and flashed a smile in her direction.

"You got company coming over?" she asked, hoping that he would say yes so, she could stick to her original plan.

Kwame shook his head and smirked, turning around to fully face her. "I will not bring no one else in here after you attacked her with a wine bottle last night."

"I could have really done damage," she warned, looking at him shrug his shoulders.

"I was hungry and if I cook, I'm making enough for everyone around. I'll be done in a minute, go get comfortable." His statement was final while he ignored hers. He was aware of how much damage she could cause.

Nadia looked at him oddly before she pulled herself away and disappeared down the hall. Tossing her bags on the bed, she kicked her sandals off and hopped into the shower. After getting out and oiling down, she put on a swimsuit and a beach dress. She would probably do a few laps in the pool after her dinner settled. It would trigger peaceful sleep, and that's exactly what she wanted. Letting her natural curls free and fall over her face, she shook them loose with her hands as she walked out of the room.

"So, what is this?" she asked, sitting at the counter studying the plate he placed in front of her. "Smells good."

"It's pineapple salmon," he spoke up, looking at her look

at her plate. He took in her wild natural hair and her make-up free face. It was beautiful. Before he got caught staring, he cleared his throat and sat across from her.

Nadia looked at the salmon perfectly plated on top of fresh pineapple spirals and mixed greens. "Thank you, you didn't have to."

Kwame shrugged his shoulders and started to eat. "It's no biggie."

Nadia couldn't remember the last time someone cooked for her besides her mother. Pouring a glass of wine, she smiled into the glass as she drunk it so he wouldn't see it. If this was what the next day and a half would be like, she was going to be a lot nicer to him than she wanted to.

After dinner, Kwame took over the cleaning of the kitchen and Nadia traveled outside to the patio with a glass in her hand. She curled up in a chair and watched the people below enjoy their bonfire. From what she could see there were three couples and they were having a great time laughed and drinking. Enjoying people watching, she didn't even hear Kwame step out on the patio. He leaned over the railing and looked down the beach at what held Nadia's attention.

"You want to crash the party?" His smile was sly, and he turned to look at her. She shook her and head and chuckled.

"No, I don't know them," she objected.

"But we could."

"But those are couples. I'm not trying to intrude on that."

Kwame chuckled, walked in the house to grab an unopened bottle of wine, two plastic wine cups and walked back on the patio. "Come on. Live life on the wild side for one night. They don't have to know anything that we don't tell them. Or you can sit up here all night and stare at them.

It's up to you. I know you didn't come to Catalina to stare at people."

"Nah, I actually came to get away from you," she quipped, making him grunt lowly before he smiled.

"Well, you failed at that so come on." Kwame outstretched his hand to help her up but in true Nadia fashion, she helped herself up and gathered the bottom of her dress in her hands and started walking down the stairs toward the beach. Shaking his head at her stubbornness, he watched as she slowly trailed in front of him. He caught up just in time to stop at the bonfire.

Kwame was far more outgoing than Nadia was. She was guarded and skeptical of everything and everyone. Kwame draped his arm over her shoulder and smirked softly at how her body tensed up when she felt his touch. "How y'all doing?"

The group looked up at them and smiled. "We're up there, we saw y'all from the patio—"

Kwame couldn't even finish his statement before one of the guys waved them over. "Come on, join in. This wasn't planned at all. We met them at the coffee shop earlier. The more, the merrier."

Kwame turned his head into Nadia's curls and pressed his lips against her temple. "See...light work."

The only reason Kwame still had all his teeth in his mouth was because they were in front of strangers and she wasn't going to jail tonight. "Mmm...I see."

😹 6 🦎

6

Nadia Garrett

SHE SAT down by Kwame and crossed her legs over one another. It was killing her to tell the group they impeded on, that they were not together. Before she could open her mouth, Kwame grabbed her hand and kissed her knuckles. He was going to lay this lie on thick. It was going to make her sick if he put his lips on her again. Letting her cashmere hand go, he poured her a cup of wine and handed it over. At least the alcohol would make this easier to deal with.

"I'm Rick and that's my wife Sharon," the guy who invited them to sit down, spoke up holding his wife's hand.

The couples went around in a circle introducing themselves. "Danny, and this is my wife Tonya."

"Jack, and my wife Pam," the last couple waved and smiled at Kwame and Nadia.

Kwame smiled wide, taking Nadia's tiny hand back in his. He was getting too much joy out of this. "Kwame, and my wife Nadia."

It wasn't a complete lie; they have always been told that they argue like an old married couple.

"You two look so amazing together," Sharon spoke up, looking at the two of them. "How long have you two been together?"

Kwame smirked at feeling Nadia squeeze his hand, warning him not to say anything but he enjoyed riling her up as much as he could. He wondered how the night would go if she were drunk and riled up. How many drinks would she not give a fuck anymore and go with the flow?

He looked at her and stared into her eyes for a moment. The way her irises contracted and switched hues when he looked at them, sent chills over his body. "What would you say? Junior year at UCLA?"

"They don't care about that," she laughed over his gaze and clenched her thighs slightly and cleared her throat.

"She was walking through the courtyard with her friends and I saw her. I knew at first, she wasn't really feeling me like that but I worked my magic," Kwame smiled wide while Nadia cut her eyes at him, remembering that day vividly.

"He was trying too hard. He usually does but it's just how he is," she replied, going along with Kwame's foolishness.

The women aww'd. Nadia let a small smile creep across her face as he kissed her knuckles again. "Not as hard as you thought?"

"I can see the love between you two," Pam cooed,

making Nadia gulp her wine down and hand the cup back over to Kwame.

"Me too, it's all over them," Sharon smiled, laying her head on her husband's shoulder.

Nadia cleared her throat as Kwame let her hand go to pour her another cup. "Enough about us, what about you guys?"

Shifting the conversation off of them to the other couples, Nadia and Kwame both listened to their stories. Nadia was four glasses in, and she was starting to feel the wine. The couples were holding hands, kissing faces, and sitting on laps. She didn't want Kwame to get any ideas or to throw her inhibitions and actually like being his company. Excusing herself from the group, she started down the beach. Kwame wasn't too far behind her after he thanked them for a great night and their hospitality.

By the time he caught up with her, she was wiping her face and staring at the ocean. Seeing the happiness oozing from the couples, her mind started running off to places where she had to pull herself out of. Nadia wanted it all and it was becoming exhausting to act as though like having someone to share life with was a farfetched idea. The only people she'd ever built a meaningful relationship with were her girls. They were happily married with kids, getting married and starting a family, and she had nothing but her pieces that she was trying as hard as she could to put together. Every day she woke up alone, she slowly accepted that this could be her forever.

Nadia could sense Kwame's presence approach her. She quickly wiped her face and looked down at her feet. "You good?"

She nodded her head yes, refusing to look at him. She wrapped her arms around herself and sighed before looking back at the sun fully disappearing over the horizon. Nadia felt Kwame get closer. He knew that his touch was unwelcomed, but he knew it was what she needed. He wrapped her up in his arms. Surprisingly, she didn't fight him. She tensed up but after a few minutes, she relaxed and let her head rest on his chest. He wasn't going to pry, instead he was going to take in this moment. It could be the first and the last.

The wind blew her hair into his face, sweeping it over to her right shoulder and he held her tighter. Bending his neck to kiss her bare shoulder, she still didn't flinch. She was in deep thought. He would have killed to get inside her head and find out what she consumed herself with. Her body was here but she was off in her sea of thoughts. Placing another kiss to her shoulder after another, he finally broke her out her thoughts. Nadia tilted her head to look at him. He let her go enough to turn around and look up at him. He examined her sad eyes and wrapped her up again with one hand. With the other, he placed it gently around her neck and pecked her lips. She didn't move; it's was like she needed to feel his touch, so she welcomed it.

Kissing her soft lips again, this time he slipped his tongue in her mouth. Nadia placed her hands on his waist and kissed him back. Kwame engulfed her in his arms and kissed her slowly and sensually. The type of kiss a girl dreamt about. The type of kiss that made her thighs clench as tight as they could. That would be the only thing to keep her standing upright and not giving up her fight. The only thing either of them could hear was the sound of the crashing ocean against the shore and the smacking of their lips.

Kwame's hand roamed down to her ass and the other gripped her hair. He pulled her hair enough to make them part lips. Nadia opened her drunken eyes and looked up at him. Instantly, biting her hip she stepped out his hold. Sucking in the night and releasing it she couldn't find the words to say. Instead, she wrapped her arms back around herself and walked back off toward the villa, leaving him standing there to bite his lip and shake his head.

"What were you thinking?" she fussed to herself as she made her way back. When she got back to the villa, she pulled her clothes off and started packing up. She felt something and it scared the hell out of her. It scared her to the point that she needed to get home in her own space to process what just happened. There was no way in hell that she actually felt anything but hate and irritation for that man. If anything, she had the wine to blame. She showered, scanned the room and set her alarm so she could catch the first ferry off the island.

Nadia could barely sleep. Every time she closed her eyes, she felt his lips and hands all over her. The feeling he enticed was electric and she was petrified. Morning couldn't come fast enough. She needed to run as far as she could, as fast as she could. Nadia needed to be sure that she would never be left alone with him again.

Her alarm went off and she was still wide awake. She was sure to leave as quietly as she could. Once she was off the ferry and in her Uber back to her home, she sighed in relief. Arriving home, she dragged her things inside, set her alarm, took a shower and melatonin and laid in the middle of her bed; trying to think about anything put Kwame and the way he looked at her. Before she drifted off, she made a mental note to let Brielle and Wren have it because there was no way that Isabella thought about all of this on her own.

7

Kwame Franklin

Kwame lied in his bed and stared at the ceiling. Since leaving Catalina, he could only think about how Nadia ran off. Not only ran from him but left like a thief in the night without so much as a fuck off. It was really messing with his head. He broke down one wall just to be met with another. He knew that getting to her wasn't going to be easy, but Kwame was used to everything folding out exactly how he wanted them to.

Unable to sleep or think about anything else but her, he sat up and turned the tv on. Grabbing his phone off of his dresser, he scrolled through his contact and hovered his finger over her name.

One text won't hurt. He was talking himself into to

doing what his heart was pushing him to do. His gut turned, feeling like a teenage boy with a crush on the popular girl at school. The words to say to her were fleeting. It was almost better at this point to return to working on her nerves. At least then he knew exactly what he was to expect. He couldn't handle this. He couldn't handle thinking she would never come back around. In the name of protecting herself from feeling, he feared that she would shut down and if she did, she would shut him out. He didn't want that. If anything, he needed Nadia to realize that since the day he saw her in the courtyard, he wanted nothing more than to be in her space.

Deciding against calling or texting her, he dropped the phone on his lap and turned to ESPN. The night had quickly turned into the morning and he was greeted by warm rays of sun through the shades of his master bedroom. Kwame didn't feel lonely in his home until now. Stretching across the bed and feeling nothing but cool sheets and pillows. Grunting lowly, he pushed himself out the bed and shuffled downstairs to the kitchen where Imelda was hard at work.

When he learned that he was relocating, he sweet-talked Imelda and her family into coming along. She would've jumped at the opportunity even if he hadn't secured a home and a bonus for her. There would be no one else he wanted to work for him but her. And Imelda didn't want to work for anyone but him. Over the years they built a strong working relationship and Kwame considered her to be family.

"How was your trip?" she asked, fluffing the pillows on the couch. Kwame shrugged his shoulders and made his way to the fridge to get a bottle of water. "That bad?"

"Nah, just wasn't long enough," he shared, leaning on the counter. "I thought I gave you the week off?"

"I thought you were going to be gone for at least another day. I didn't know if you were going to bring that lady friend home or not...so I thought I would tidy up," Imelda shared as she finished beating the life back into one set of pillows and moving across the open living room to another couch.

Kwame winced at the thought of how Nadia got his weekend guest to leave so quickly. It was that shit that she would do to make him want to snatch her up but at the same time, he enjoyed it. Her relation to the women he brought around was always dramatic. His mind trailed off on how Nadia had never brought any man around him and probably never would. Kwame couldn't remember anyone other than Vinny that she was actually into. The list was short. After learning her story, he could understand why.

"Well, she made a quick exit," he mumbled, topping the top to his water bottle and bringing in to his lips. "Very, very, quick."

There wasn't anything he could say or do that would get his mind off of Nadia and how she left him standing on the beach dumbfounded. If anything, the more he thought about the hint of lingering wine she left on his lips before she ran away, only irritated him more. The more he thought about her wrapped up in his arms, the scent of her hair in the breeze. The way she looked in her natural state. The way she trusted him if it were only for a moment was liable to drive him insane. It all made him replay what happened over again on a loop. Kwame had no intentions of kissing her, but he was overtaken. He waited almost seven years to taste her lips.

Her lips.

They were soft as a feather, thick enough to suck on and

juicy just like he thought they would taste. Since having a taste, there was a fire ignited that would be hell to put out. Everything he was feeling was rushing over him. It took an extensive amount of control to not chase after her and scoop her up in his arms and make this final. But Nadia wasn't ready for him yet. He would have to practice an extreme amount of patience in order to finally break her down.

He didn't know how much strength he had in him. He only had two options. He could work like a crack addict and break her down, show her that the protection she gave herself could be found in his embrace. The love she pretended that she didn't need was in his touch. Or he could fuck her out of his system. Although he's been doing it for years and it yielded no worthy results. All he had was his first option. Kwame had to step up and show her that a man's touch shouldn't be one that she was fearful of.

But before he could do that, he needed to look at himself. In order to end this war between them and present himself to her, he had to clean up the ugly shit that he buried deep under the surface. All his wounds and fear of commitment had to go. Nadia wasn't a woman who was going to be accepting of half of a man. She wasn't going to be taking anyone else's shit either, especially because she had enough on her own and prided herself on being able to take care of herself. It would be a new day for both of them when she wasn't in control of that anymore.

The doorbell rang, snapping Kwame out of his thoughts. Standing up, he walked over to the door and pulled it open to see Julian and Roman standing on the other side with grins plastered across their faces. Taking the opportunity to press his lips together, Kwame shut the door in their faces and walked away. By the time he plopped down on the couch that Imelda just finished beating the life back into, they helped themselves in.

"Damn is that how we get greeted?" Julian questioned, faking like his feelings were actually hurt.

"Ew," Roman said, looking over Kwame's demeanor. "You look salty as hell nigga. I thought Catalina was supposed to relax you?"

Kwame cut his eyes at them as Julian sat down and Roman walked into the kitchen. "Do you have a tapeworm?" Julian asked, watching Roman go through the fridge. "You're worse than an unwanted houseguest."

"He is an unwanted houseguest," Kwame mumbled. "What do y'all want?"

"Damn, Black Knight," Roman kissed his teeth, closing the fridge. "You don't have shit to eat. Everything is green."

"You should try it, it might make you grow a few inches taller," Kwame quipped, dropping his head back on the pillows.

"We just came to see how your trip was. The girls are headed to brunch, so we thought we'd pop in," Julian smirked at Kwame, who bounced his eyes back and forth between the two of them.

Kwame kissed his teeth and palmed his face. "I don't know whether to knock y'all heads clean off your shoulders or not. You niggas set me up!"

"What?" they both gasped in unison, as if they didn't know about anything that was taking place in Catalina.

Julian smirked slyly and looked at Kwame's bothered posture as he stared at the ceiling. "Why would we ever do such a thing?"

"I don't know. Maybe because y'all are hell and terrible ass friends," Kwame grumbled and looked at them. "Y'all really could've given me a heads up. You know that crazy ass girl threw a bottle at my date for the weekend?"

"Why the hell would you bring someone with you?" Roman asked, flailing his arms in the air before popping the top to a green smoothie Kwame had in the fridge. Taking a huge gulp, he instantly regretted it and spit out the contents into the sink. "That shit is disgusting."

"Would you quit and clean my shit up!" Kwame fussed at him. "Don't bring his ass over here anymore. And yes, Nadia's crazy ass threw a bottle at the girl."

"Well, what was the girl doing that would cause her to get hit with a bottle?" Julian asked, narrowing his eyes over at Kwame. He knew the answer involved him being in a compromising position. "I know for a fact that Nadia doesn't miss."

"I was getting some head in the foyer." Kwame shrugged and Roman and Julian groaned in irritation. "I don't know why you two are so frustrated with this. I was the one that had to share my space with her for a day and a half."

"Nigga, because we're sick of y'all being at each other's throats. We were sure that you would be able to take care of it, but you have failed us." Roman his shook head and hummed. "Mm mm mm. I got to say I thought you had more juice."

"Tiny Tim, I am the juice god. She is just ..." Kwame sucked in some air through his nostrils and shook his head. "She's ..."

"Spit it out. She's what?" Julian asked, snapping his fingers.

"A damn pain in my ass. It was like pulling teeth. I'll be happy if I don't see her for a while."

"I've never seen nobody lie like he does," Julian groaned, shaking his head. "Y'all didn't even reach a resolve, nothing? So, we are going to be subjected to another seven years of torture if no one comes and scoops her ass up?"

"Scooping who up for what?" Kwame asked, looking at Julian like he was crazy. Kwame was not with the idea of having any man swoop and do shit. "Ain't no nigga scooping up nothing. Believe that."

8

Nadia Garrett

SLEEP WAS SLOWLY RELEASING its hold off of her. Stretching across her bed, she looked around her room and groaned. Nadia quickly realized that she wasn't in Catalina anymore and the reality bothered her. Her dramatic exit bothered her even more. While sitting up and scanning the room, she groaned lowly wanting to go back to sleep but instead, she spotted the bouquet of flowers Wren left on the nightstand. Softly smiling, Nadia pulled the card from the bouquet and scanned over Wren's handwriting.

I hope you enjoyed yourself...you deserve it.

She placed the card on the dresser by the vase of flowers and picked up her phone. Nadia had a bone to pick with them and a stomach to fill, so it only made sense to make them pick her up and go to Isabella's for brunch. She needed a girls' day to distract her from the fact that she dropped her guard for a few seconds with Kwame. What she felt was electric, uncontrolled pulses of energy running through her body. It was unfamiliar and it petrified her. She'd had her needs met here and there throughout the years, but she never had a man's touch allure such a sensation. The sensation came at the hands of Kwame which scared her even more. It took hard work and a lot of energy to detest him and the way he handled himself. She didn't want to think about him in any other capacity.

Pushing herself out of the bed, she shuffled into the bathroom and got into the shower. After a long hot shower in attempts to wash the memories of Catalina away, she got out and started to oil herself down. Nadia was enjoying having her natural hair wild and free, so she decided to leave her curls scattered about until she went back to work in a couple of days. She wasn't looking forward to being anywhere near Kwame alone. It could end up dangerous for her and any more damage to her heart would be incurable.

After pulling a pair of leggings over her toasted-caramel thighs, and a t-shirt over her head, she wrapped her hair into a bun. Focusing on getting her bun just right, the doorbell rang. Instead of going to get it she let it ring, knowing that both Brielle and Wren had a key to get in. Nadia was in no rush to get the door until the ringing became annoying.

"Seriously?" she whined, pulling herself away from the mirror and starting her pursuit down the stairs to the front door. Nadia yanked the door open, expecting to see her friends engulfed in their childish behavior. Instead, she was greeted by a box.

She squatted down to pick it up and take the top off. Looking at her surroundings, Nadia didn't see anyone around, and it instantly made her anxiety peak. Donte's words rang over and over in her mind. Nadia's eyes went from the driveway back to contents of the box and gagged at the sight of the dead rat. He knew where she lived. He was too close for comfort.

The dead rat made her mind flashback to the first time she was greeted by a dead rat on the doorstep. Just another scare tactic his used to keep her mouth shut when she was younger. Quickly covering the box, she saw Brielle's car pull into the driveway. In great attempts to keep Brielle and Wren clueless to what was going on, she sprinted down the stairs to throw the box away and calm her nerves. If she wasn't looking over her shoulder before, she definitely was looking now.

After years of being comfortable moving around the city, she now had to be a prisoner in her own home and city. The threat of Donte was unsettling, and it made her want to shut down. But if she did, she would ruin all the progress she'd made over the few months.

Folding her shaking arms over her chest, she turned around and met Brielle and Wren at the front door. "You look rested," Wren smirked, lightly biting her lip and looking Nadia over. Her smirk faded, catching the terrified look etched into her eyebrows.

"What's wrong?" Wren asked as Brielle hopped out of her car and joined the two on the steps. "What's going on?"

"Nothing," Nadia lied, forcing a smile to spread across her lips. "It was just a rodent. I have to call the exterminator."

"Mm," Brielle rose her brow and studied Nadia's body language. "If you say so...I thought you would be ready when we got here. I'm hungry."

"She's been whining about food the whole way over

here," Wren rolled her eyes and stepped into the house. Nadia traveled into the house behind them and closed and locked the door behind them.

"I just need to grab my purse and my shoes. I already told Izzy that we're on our way," Nadia shared, heading up the stairs to get her purse, gun, and to slide some sandals on her feet. She normally didn't carry her gun, but with Donte lurking around in the shadows, she needed to stay as ready as she could.

Returning to the group, Nadia nodded her head toward the door. "Come on, let's go."

Wren was still very skeptical about her behavior. She made a mental note to make a comment about it later. Wren knew that Nadia always had a reason for not coming outright and saying what was bothering her. Brielle and Wren marched out the door as Nadia set the alarm to the house. Hopefully, a few mimosas and couple pieces of French toast would ease her active nerves.

Nadia was silent the entire ride to the restaurant for brunch. It was until she was settled at the table and Isabella came out of the kitchen with a couple of bottles of champagne, ice buckets, and orange juice. Nadia turned her attention from watching the cameras of the house on her phone to Isabella. Isabella smiled wide at the trio. "Well…"

"Well, we've been waiting to hear the details too…" Wren spoke up, getting Nadia's attention.

Nadia looked over them and pinched her brows together. "After I kicked Kwame and his hoe of the weekend out after getting head in the foyer, I figured you three were behind that foolery. Stop staring at me, there is nothing to talk about."

Brielle, Isabella, and Wren smacked their teeth simultaneously and rolled their eyes. "You cannot tell me that three days away from everything, everyone, the beach, and your skimpy bikini got you nothing at all," Wren groaned and slapped her forehead.

"I don't know what would possess you three to attempt to force us together," Nadia squinted her eyes and looked over them. "Who came up with the idea to put Nadia and Kwame in the same space for three days and think that we would somehow write a love story?"

Wren shifted her eyes over at Brielle and Isabella and looked back at Nadia. "I just thought that after all these years, you and my bull-headed brother would just crash into each other and all the nonsense would be done."

Brielle poured herself on a mimosa and released a sigh. "We are sick of you two at each other's throats all the time."

"You are sure a hopeless romantic," Nadia responded as Isabella took a seat by her. "I will do all you guys one better. I won't say two words to the name. I will do my job and go home. I have ignored him before and I can do it again."

Brielle tilted her head to the side and squinted her eyes in hopes that she could read Nadia clearly. "Something happened between you two, didn't it?"

Isabella and Wren stared at Nadia, waiting for her to answer. Instead, she propped her chin in the palm of her hand and looked at them. "I threw a bottle at him and his freak of the week...after that, there is nothing else to talk about. He went his way and I went mine."

"I swear to God," Isabella rubbed her temples and hummed lowly. "I'm fresh out of ideas to get you two together."

"Why is there a need to put me together with anyone? I've told you guys once, twice and three times but I'll tell you one last time. I don't want it. I am okay with the idea of being alone. Let's save you all the time and me the aggravation...can we eat and talk about something else now?" Nadia reached over Isabella to pour herself a mimosa while Brielle and Wren sighed heavily.

"Is there something else that's bothering you? You've been off since we pulled up?" Brielle asked concerned, watching Nadia make a mimosa that was nine-ninety percent champagne.

"Nope," she lied. "Everything is good."

It was damaging the way Nadia thought that shutting down would keep everyone at an arm's length and them from worrying about her. The only thing it did was raise red flags for everyone. She needed them and her fear of them getting hurt along with her, but she wouldn't let them in to help her through this.

"I think he got to her," Brielle whispered to Wren, making Isabella giggle.

"He will not touch me with a ten-foot pole."

9

Nadia Garrett

THE OFFICE WALL was adorned with degrees from every university she could think of. Every session, Nadia found another degree and another award. She normally focused on everything else when she was proposed with a question that she either didn't want to answer, or the answer was too difficult to process. Her three-day escape wasn't long enough to be sitting here and dealing with her emotions. On top of everything else, she now had to deal with the seed that Kwame planted on her lips and on her spirit.

"Nadia," Yvette pulled Nadia out of space and back to the discussion. "You're doing it again."

Nadia dragged her eyes away from the wall and back to

Yvette sitting across from her with her legs crossed and her ebony eyes fixed on her. "What were you asking me?"

"When was the last time you talked to your mother?" Yvette repeated her question. She watched Nadia's chest rise and drop.

"I haven't since the last time I went to Oakland. But that's not what's bothering me..." Nadia shared, closing her eyes and clenching them as tight as she could, trying not to break down. "He's back and he won't leave me alone."

Yvette let the silence fall between them and waited until Nadia was ready to continue. "Before I left for my trip, he texted me and when I got back, he left a dead rat on my step. The first time he left a rat on my doorstep was after I threatened to tell my mother what he was doing. He is too close to me. I don't know what to do. I don't feel safe in my own home."

"Why haven't you told anyone?" Yvette asked, leaning up and looking at Nadia. "This is the reason you have people who love you."

"I've always been the one protecting them. I don't want anyone mixed up in my shit. They have families and a life to live. I'm not going to interrupt that with my stuff. That's not fair to them."

Yvette hummed. "So, let me get this right...your friends can pile their burdens on you. You support them through it and you're there every step of the way...why won't you let them be your support?"

Nadia slowly lifted her head and sniffled. "I don't know how..."

"Nadia, you cannot take on the world by yourself. I know you think you can, but you can't. It will not end well. This is a dangerous situation and you are going to need your friends to help you through it. Stop trying to be your own hero, it's okay for someone to save you every once in a while."

Nadia nodded her head and wiped her face. "I'll try."

"Make it a point. Okay?"

"Okay." Nadia stood up and adjusted her dress before Yvette hugged her. "Thank you."

"Call me if you need me. You are not going through this alone, we got you," Yvette assured before Nadia left her office.

Her phone started to ring on the way to the car. Everything had been silent since she left Kwame in Catalina, so she wasn't surprised that he was having his assistant call her. When it came to the business of the restaurants, Kwame always called her himself. If she were being completely honest, she missed his voice. Refusing to dwell on it, she answered the phone.

"Hello." Nadia cleared her throat as she reached her car and unlocked the door.

"Good afternoon, Ms. Garrett, how is everything going?" Amanda asked just as chipper as she wanted to be. She was always happy which made Nadia wonder where the hell she had that bottled up sunshine hidden, and if it was natural or drug induced.

"I'm good Amanda, yourself?" Nadia climbed into her car and locked the doors. The minute she asked the question, she regretted it because Amanda fired off.

"Well, my cat ran away last week, and I've been driving myself crazy trying to find her. This has been my third time losing her. Thank God I don't have kids because I can't even keep my cat," Amanda shared, making Nadia's head spin and her lip curl up.

She would have rather Kwame call with a sarcastic tone

than listen to another moment of Amanda's cat chronicles. "Okay, so what's up?"

"Oh yeah, the reason I called,' Amanda chuckled. "Mr. Franklin needs you to meet him and Isabella in Arizona tomorrow to view a few properties last minute. He knows it's last minute but he told me to tell you that he didn't want to okay anything without you. I've already booked your first-class flight, it leaves at eight. I'm also sending over your hotel reservation. You'll be staying at the Four Seasons in Scottsdale. I also checked the radar, and it's going to be hot so pack light clothes."

Amanda was thorough, Nadia couldn't deny that. "How long are we going to be there?"

"Uh, Mr. Franklin said it shouldn't be longer than two days, but you should prepare for three. The list of properties will be sent with everything else. The car will be at your house to get you at six," Amanda added with a delightful sigh at the end of her response.

"Okay," Nadia spoke up, following by a sigh of her own. "I'll head home and get packed up. Thanks for the call, I'll be looking for your email and I hope you find your cat."

"Thank you, Nadia," she smiled through the phone before she disconnected their call.

Nadia pulled out of the parking lot and headed home to repack her bags and get ready for her flight this afternoon. Brielle and Wren were on the phone while she packed her bag for the next few days. "He must be mad at you if he had Amanda call you."

Nadia shook her head at Wren's comment. She could deny it all she wanted but she knew it was true. He was probably fuming about the way she left after the moment they shared.

"All I have to say is don't get arrested in Scottsdale...it's too hot for me to be coming out there and bailing you out," Brielle hummed.

"It's not going to be any of that," Nadia shared, throwing her flat iron in the suitcase. "I just wanted you guys to know what was going on. I have about forty minutes to be ready to get out of here. I'll text you two when I land. Love ya!"

"Love ya!"

Hearing the call end, Nadia finished packing her bag and double-checked to make sure she had everything she needed. The minute she slid her feet into her sandals the doorbell rang. Gathering her things, she traveled to the front door and set the alarm. Climbing into the back of the car, Nadia closed her eyes and gave herself a pep talk while the driver loaded her bags in the trunk.

"You're going to work, nothing personal, Nadia. Do not drop your guard."

Landing in Scottsdale, Arizona, Nadia was slapped in the face by the heat. She'd never been so happy not to have worn panties under her sundress. The car waiting on the curb was just a few steps away, but Nadia was already covered in a sheer layer of sweat. The first thing she was going to do when she got to her room, was to take a shower and go to sleep. After reviewing the schedule for tomorrow, she needed all the sleep that she could get.

When she arrived at the hotel, she was greeted warmly by the receptionist before being escorted to her room by the bellhop. "Ms. Garrett if there is anything else you need, please call."

"Thank you." After tipping the bellhop, she waited until he left the room to lock the door and look around.

A bouquet of flowers rested on the nightstand with a

bottle of Pinot Noir and a wine tray. Her smile was involuntary as she made her way across the room to read the card.

We leave at nine. Be on time - K.

Rolling her eyes, it didn't make the smile leave her face. Removing her dress and popping the cork to the bottle of wine, Nadia trailed into the bathroom and sat on the edge of the tub while it filled up. She dropped a scoop of bath salts in and inhaled the aroma released throughout the bathroom.

She needed to unwind. If she could carry her stillness over into tomorrow, she wouldn't need to constantly pray about her restraint around Kwame.

1 °

Kwame Franklin

HE WAITED for Nadia in the lobby along with Isabella. The goal was to get started at nine, try a local restaurant for lunch, and come back to eat dinner at the hotel. Kwame had two days of property tours lined up, he wanted to be sure that they found the perfect spot to set up the next chain.

Kwame was growing irritated with her tardiness. "Why can't y'all be on time for anything?"

Isabella cut he eyes at Kwame and sucked her teeth. "Listen, be nice to her. I see that my trip didn't work."

"I don't even want to talk about it. We got shit to do today and her inability to be on time is going to put us behind schedule," Kwame whined.

"You want some cheese to go with that whine, Kwame?"

Isabella snickered. "You give up too easily. I thought we talked about this. You do know if you're nicer to her that you'll get the results that you want. But if you continue to be a brut, she will shut down every time. She needs to be shown something other than men who only want to wreck her world and not build it. Be that man Kwame."

"I'm really trying but she can work my damn nerves," he groaned.

"Because you're in love with her," she smiled. "No one ever gets on your nerves more than someone you love. Deny it all you want. You've been in her space since college, to tell me you don't is to deny the very thing that makes you tick."

"Isabella, I—"

Isabella smiled and waved at Nadia stepping off the elevator and walking toward them. "Don't say nothing, she's headed this way."

Kwame looked over his shoulder and watched as Nadia floated his way. She was dressed perfectly for the heat. A pair of yellow, floral print loose flowing pants and a white tank top tucked into the top of her pants. Her hair was pressed and tucked behind her ears. He was partial to her natural appearance but with the sheer layer of makeup, she was still beautiful to him.

He stuffed his hand in his DriFit golf pants. Everything he wore was DriFit, the last thing he wanted was to be hot and deal with whatever Nadia could possibly do. Grunting at the sight of her, Isabella nudged him.

"Remember what I said. I'm going to the car."

Groaning at Isabella walking away, he refocused back on Nadia. "Nine somehow turns into nine-thirty, I see."

"For someone who books last minute business trips you should be happy I'm here," Nadia shot back with a sarcastic smirk. "Let's go."

"Why can't you just be on time?" Kwame asked, rubbing his brow.

"If it were so important, Kwame...you would have done all of this without me. But because you clearly couldn't, talk to me with some sense. I'm not with the shits today," Nadia fired off her response, making Kwame's eye twitch.

"Jesus Christ." Kwame sucked up the air as she walked past him, and out the door behind Isabella. She'd already irritated the hell out of him, and the scent of her lingering perfume was going to make it that much harder to keep his hands to himself.

Pulling himself to the car, he got in the front seat and buckled his seatbelt. "Today is going to be a great day." Isabella clasped her hands and smiled at the two. Nadia and Kwame's expressions mirrored one another.

"Don't," Nadia warned. "Let's just get through this. It's hot as hell and I don't want to be aggravated any more than I am."

"You should probably stop talking then. The amount of hot air in your lungs is going to make the temperature rise a few degrees," Kwame muttered.

Nadia kneed the back on his seat forcefully enough to make him grunt in aggravation. "Shut up, boy."

"Oh boy," Isabella groaned, rolling her eyes. "This is how it's about to go."

By the time they got to the third property space, Kwame and Nadia were at each other's necks. She said yes to something, he said no. She pushed to get something added, he pulled. The back and forth was irritating Isabella. Some much to the point that she stomped out the restaurant and back to the car.

"You two are so damn ridiculous. All I want is the best space. I know which one I want. So, this is over. I'm going back to the room. Y'all need to figure this shit out. It's fucking ridiculous that you two are grown as hell and can't even agree to disagree. I'm sick of this...I can only imagine how your friends feel!" Isabella fussed the entire way back to the hotel.

Nadia and Kwame sat silently in the car like two kids being scolded by their mother. When the car stopped in front of the hotel, Isabella couldn't hop out fast enough and rush inside the building to the bar.

"See what you did," Kwame mumbled.

"What was that?" Nadia questioned from the back seat. "See what I did? Nigga, you tripping."

"No, you're tripping. That's our client. You need to pull your shit together," Kwame groaned. He was frustrated for a number of things but none of it was how Nadia handled the events of the day because he was poking her just to get a reaction.

"No offense, but I have listened to you two go back and forth for an hour so please get out," the driver spoke up as politely as he could.

Nadia grunted and pushed the door open and climbed out. "You don't have to ask me twice."

Getting out behind her, Kwame caught up with her and caught her by the arm. "Nadia stop walking away from me dammit."

Nadia didn't think twice. The way he grabbed her made her mind flashback. Instead of pulling away from him, she slapped the taste out his mouth before storming inside. The sting and the embarrassment of the assault shot fire through Kwame. He was about to settle this once and for all.

Barreling through the lobby, he got to the elevators and blew smoke out his nostrils while he waited for the elevator to come down so he could go light Nadia up like a Christmas tree.

All he could see was red. She had pushed several buttons in his head. She had embarrassed him several times but this took the cake. This was the last and final straw. Every ounce of patience he was trying to hold on to, flew out of the window.

It felt like an eternity for the elevator to hit the ground floor. When it did, he stalked on and paced the floor until he could get off on her floor. If his chocolate skin could burn red, it would have. No one in the world could make him this mad but her. She could either apologize and get her shit together, or Kwame was backing off once and for all. He was fine before he caught feelings for her, and he would be just fine after her. At least that's what he used to convince himself; that if he forced her out of his life right now, he would be okay.

He knew it wouldn't but all he could see was the anger that only she could evoke.

Reaching her room, he pounded on the door. At this point, he didn't give a fuck who heard or saw him. After getting slapped like a bitch in front of a group of bystanders, all his cool was out the window. Nadia officially had him fucked up.

11

1 [I]

Nadia Garrett

THE BANGING on the door only indicated that Kwame was possibly on the verge of kicking the door down to knock her head off her shoulders. She didn't mean to slap him, it was just a natural reaction to him grabbing her as suddenly as he did. She chewed on her lip as she eased to the door to open it.

Pulling it open, Kwame barreled in with his nostrils flaring. He looked like a raging bull as he passed her. Before she could turn around and face him, he was standing nose-to-nose with her. "So, this is what we're going to do? Hm?"

He stared her down. Holding her gaze, he closed whatever space was left between the two of them. So close he could feel the heat radiating from her body. If he listened close enough, he could hear her heart pound against her rib cage.

Nadia looked into Kwame's eyes and tried as hard as she could to look away. She wanted to break contact with him and find words. Any words would be better than the dumbfounded expression she held at that moment. All she could do was silently study every wrinkle of his face while he stared at his violator. The only woman who made him mad as hell, but he still wanted to hold her close and kiss her face.

"Is this the game you want to play with me?" he growled at her. Kwame was unhinged. His self-control was gone, all at the hand of her. He wasn't even sure that Nadia knew the extent of the power she had over him. If she wanted him to bow down and worship her like the Holy Ghost, he would without question.

"What in the fuck is your problem? Have you lost your fucking mind? You clearly have!" He backed her into the wall and continued to glare down at her. Kwame's beard-covered jaw clenched tightly, and he gritted his teeth. He wanted her to have the same energy she did outside of the lobby when she slapped hellfire out of him.

The longer he glared at her the more he wanted to knock some sense into her but just as furious as she made him, she turned him on. Nadia was going to pay for every time she said something out the way to him. But ultimately, she was going to pay for being unable to keep her hands to herself.

"Get away from me," Nadia finally grunted, pushing him away from her. Kwame overpowered her. It didn't matter how hard or how many times she pushed, Kwame didn't budge. Instead, he grabbed her wrist and pinned them to her side.

"Fuck no. You can't keep your fucking hands to yourself and that's a problem for me."

"Well, then take your problem and go away," Nadia squirmed, trying to get out of his hold but there was no use. He had her pinned against the wall. "Get off of me Kwame!"

"No! I am so sick of your mouth." His mouth hovered over hers and the heaving of his chest intensified. "But I can show you better than I can tell you."

"You're not going to do shit. Now get off of me and get out," she grunted, still trying to get out of his hold. "Are you done?"

"Nadia, your mouth is going to get you fucked up," he grunted, jolting her enough to get her to shut up. Nadia's eye's widened, quickly realizing that Kwame wasn't playing with her. The games were over, and she'd spun a web that she couldn't get out of.

He was going to finish what he started in Catalina and there was only one way she was going to get out of it. She couldn't deny that this was what she wanted to happen. Her window for Kwame to be soft and gentle with her was gone. It left when she ran away from him. She could never bring herself to admit that she wanted him. All the years of watching him parade around with other women irritated her, but who was she to demand his love and affection.

Nadia anxiously licked her bottom lip with the tip of her tongue, in anticipation of feeling his lips on hers again. To deny that she wanted him was to deny the throbbing happening at the meeting of her thighs. She had fantasized about his touch since that night she left him on the beach. She could never bring herself to say it out loud, but his touch was the only one that she wanted to mimic time and time again. She could only think about the way his skin would feel against her skin. How she would scream his name while her nails clawed into his back.

She shuddered slightly before Kwame could take her lips into his. Hungrily kissing her, he pressed his waist against hers so she could feel the check her smart ass wrote and was about to cash. He didn't release her hands; he only interlocked his fingers with hers and squeezed them lightly.

Kwame kissed her face, her lips, her neck, her shoulders and back to her lips. He wasn't going to rush this, but he was going to make sure that he drove her as crazy as she drove him.

Uncontrollably, Nadia moaned as Kwame kissed her collar bone. His kisses were rough like he'd been starved, and she was his last meal. Each kiss to her skin left a mark. Some faint and some bright red. When this was over, he wanted...he needed her to remember the lesson she learned. Kwame couldn't let her moans distract him from the task at hand while he worked his mouth down to her breasts. Each time he reached a zone that made her moan, he started all over again. He was going to put something on her that would have her screaming his name by the time the night was over.

Nadia clamped down on her lip as she welcomed Kwame's warm mouth on her erect nipple. Her nipples were her erogenous zone. If he were looking for a reaction out of her that was one area that would cause her levy to break. She couldn't fight him if she wanted to. She knew her ass was in trouble and the only option she had was to suck it up and take her ass whipping like the woman she was.

Trying not to release a moan, she did. Only for Kwame, she normally didn't praise her lovers in the way she was trying not to praise him. Every kiss to her skin proved that he was worthy of it. It only made him suck on her nipple harder. Wrapping his arms around her waist, he pulled her away from the wall and propped her up on the couch, where her double D's could sit in his face and he could have his way with them. He only went over this moment a million times in his head. Sucking her breast like they were the giver of life, her moans turned up a little higher.

From her breast, he trailed his tongue down her stomach to the top of her pants. Tearing them at the seam as he yanked them off, he smirked at the sight of her lace thong cradling her flower. Hooking his finger under the top of the fabric, he pulled it upward and applied pressure against her clitoris that made her moan and squirm. He kept it up until her body was damn near begging to be taken by him. "Please, don't tease me."

Her center throbbed. Locking eyes with her, he smirked and licked his lips.

Tearing her panties off, he tossed them to the side and smiled at her pussy lips. They glistened under the dim light like they possessed a foreign power. She wanted him as bad as he wanted her. His dick was pressing against his pants, begging to come out. As bad as he wanted to bury himself inside of her walls, he was going to make her beg.

Nadia moaned, feeling the thickness of his tongue run over her folds. Kwame spread her legs wide and forcefully held them down. "Don't move."

"Mmm," she hummed, holding her breasts in her hands.

She was sweet against his tongue, so sweet that it made him groan while he pulled her bud out through the petals. Nadia's center was super sensitive, and she was trying her best not to feel overwhelmed by his touch. Any sexual encounters prior to this were nothing compared to him and he hadn't even made her cum yet. Nadia was used to being in control and she couldn't contain herself or wrap her mind around what was happening. All she knew is that she wanted more of him and whatever feeling he was pulling from her.

Just a moment ago she was pinned against the wall, now she was spread open on the couch, rushing like Niagara Falls. How could someone she couldn't stand and spent years hating, be the one to command these reactions from her body? No man had ever made her cum so quickly and look forward to another after another. Kwame's tongue left a puddle under her that grew larger by the second.

Kwame slurped up juices to quench his thirst and let go of her shaking legs. Scooping her up, he carried her to the room and gently dropped her on the bed. Stepping out of his clothes, he kept his eyes on her. "Don't move."

Nadia watched as Kwame freed himself from his boxer briefs. Her eyes widened, and she bit her bottom lip. She now knew why he talked shit the way he did. He had the length, girth, and mean ass hook to make it up. Instantly, she regretted laying her hands on him and any other slick shit she let off her tongue during the day.

Kwame held his dick proudly and shook it lightly. It was dripping and pulsating, eager to whip her into shape and she was eager to feel his touch again. "Spread em," Kwame ordered, pushing her legs open with his knees while he climbed on top. Complying to his orders, she felt the pressure of him at her opening.

Nadia prided herself on never running, but she backed away from him unsure if she could handle the gift he had. "Don't run now. You did that already. That running shit is done."

Gasping as he inched his way inside of her, Nadia's eyes rolled into the back of her head. She was consumed with pleasure and pain. She didn't know whether to tap out or show him how sorry she was and fuck him back. It was her natural instinct to press her hand against his waist to keep him from going any deeper. Kwame grabbed her chin gently and looked at her in the eyes. "Move your fucking hand."

Kwame took her hand and sucked on her fingers before he pinned them over her head. He slowly pumped in and out of her honey pot, so she could get accustomed to his size. Watching her body relax, he loosened up his grip on her arms letting her bury her nails into his flesh. Nadia's hips rocked against his motion; her legs locked around his waist and she moaned his name in his ear.

Kwame planted his face in the nook of her neck. Sucking on her neck, her juices coated his cocoa-dipped rod. "You feel like home," his husky voice grunted in her ear, making her wetter with every pump.

Nadia gripped the sheets for dear life as Kwame picked up his speed and rose to his knees. Placing his hand above her pelvis, he wanted to grace her g-spot and make her levy overflow. Now that she was adjusted, he was going to tag her walls like graffiti. He didn't need to tell her that now she was his.

Their bodies were drenched in sweat, entangled into one knot. She couldn't tell where his ended and hers began. Nadia's natural hair and clip in no longer blended. "Turn over."

She did, biting her lip and gripping the sheets and she couldn't control her moans. "Shit," she moaned into the pillow while putting a dip into her back, feeling Kwame reenter her temple and crash his body into hers.

Pulling on her hair, he felt the clip-ins and pulled them out. Nadia held her head up, still biting into the pillow. "Oh my God."

"Are you going to hit me again?"

"Noooo," she moaned, completely overtaken by his euphoria.

"I can't hear you, baby speak up."

"No, I'm sor—shit! I'm going to cum again."

Kwame held on to her hips as tight as he could. Nadia started fucking him back and he was going to bite a hole in his lip while he held onto her. "Bust that shit open."

Smacking her ass, he felt her body tighten around him and shake. "Fuck!" Nadia moaned into the pillow, feeling Kwame release his warmth. When he pulled out, she laid still to try to regain some of her strength. Spending the night or falling asleep after sex was never her thing. It was second nature to get up and leave.

Kwame pushed his body out the bed and shuffled into the bathroom. After a couple of minutes, he returned with a warm towel and wiped Nadia's face, neck, breast, inner thighs, and swollen flower off from their session. She had underestimated him and now she trying to come up with her exit strategy. Kwame could read her mind and scoffed lightly. "Don't even try to walk or run away. You're not going to make it. Stay in the moment and enjoy."

"I can't feel my legs," she lowly whined, watching his every moment. She watched as he wiped himself down and then tossed the towel into the basket in the bathroom.

"Every time you take a step, you'll be reminded to never do that shit again." Kwame wrapped his arms around her and pulled her closer to him. Positioning his body between her legs, he placed an affectionate kiss to her lips before laying his head on her stomach. "Get some sleep. You're going to need it."

1²

Nadia Garrett

KWAME WASN'T BLUFFING when he said that she was going to feel the remnants of his work from the night before. Every inch of her body was sore; every time she took a step, she winced lowly. Even though she was sore and damn near remorseful that she put her hands on him, she would probably do it again just to feel their bodies as one.

Laying her head on the side of the tub, she didn't bother lifting her head up when Kwame walked into the bathroom. "You good?" He knew the answer, he only asked so he could smile at her reaction.

Waking up to her was the highlight of his morning. Then breakfast in bed, then room service delivering breakfast in bed. Kwame had waited almost seven years to get his hands on Nadia, and now that he had a grip, he wasn't letting up.

Nadia tiredly raised her middle finger out the water and sighed. "As good as it gets. Is there going to be a conversation about this? Or can I pretend that it never happened."

Kwame chuckled and kissed the top of her head. "Baby, you'll never forget me."

"You are so cocky, it's sickening," she groaned, moving her leg in the water. "I'm not going to able to walk for days."

"Nadia, you caused that on yourself. Had your ass just stayed put in Catalina, you would be able to walk right now," Kwame spoke up, admiring how she lazily rested in the tub of water. "Stop running from me."

Nadia looked up and him and tilted her head. "You've never given me anything to run to." The look Kwame gave her made her clench her thighs and groan, feeling the pressure on her swollen flower.

"When you get back to Cali, let me know you made it safely. Isabella found the space she wants. I'm going to sign the paperwork." Kwame squatted down on the side of the tub and lifted her chin. Tenderly kissing her lips, he smirked softly. "Don't forget."

Nadia clamped down on her lip and watched as he stood back to his feet and pulled himself away from her. Once she heard the door close to the room, she groaned and slid herself under the water.

What the fuck have you gotten yourself into?

After dragging around the hotel room, gathering her things, she stepped back and looked at the room. Scanning the area, a smile crossed her face, remembering how Kwame took control completely. The positions he put her in, the shit he talked and could back up, all made her bite her lip, inhale and release a moan. The light tapping at the door broke her out of the trance he still had looming over her. Moving slowly to the door, she pulled it open and stepped out of the way to let the bellhop grab her bags and escort her down to the car waiting in front of the hotel.

"Ms. Garrett, I hope you enjoyed your stay and we'll see you next time," he smiled warmly at her after handing her bags over to the driver. Helping her into the car, Nadia smiled and slid into the car carefully.

"Thank you." Snaking her phone out of her purse, she spotted a few texts from Wren about tonight. Somehow some way, Nadia was going to have to act as though Kwame hadn't given her the best ride of her life.

Every time she thought about how his hands connected with her body, she wanted another hit. She was partially upset with herself for giving in to him but yielding to him for the time was more rewarding than the first. She was consumed by the thought of him the entire flight. Eventually, the two of them would have to talk about what the hell this was. Until then, she was going to continue riding this high.

She arrived home just in time for Brielle and Wren to bombard her kitchen with food and champagne. Nadia had to pop an Advil just so she could walk without raising their brows.

"How was Scottsdale?" Wren asked, popping the cork on the champagne. "Izzy find another spot?"

"She did. The paperwork should be signed by now," Nadia spoke up, wincing lowly as she sat at the table. "I have never walked so much in my damn life."

"I'm not surprised, Kwame is a walking billboard for fitness. It's aggravating," Wren rolled her eyes. "You should make him pay for a spa treatment."

"Nah," Nadia declined, shaking her head and frowning

her face. "I got us kicked out the car by the driver and Isabella cursed us out. Sooo, I'm good."

Brielle turned around to look at her and shook her head. "I don't want to know. I got something to tell y'all..."

"You're pregnant?" Nadia and Wren asked in unison.

Brielle chewed her lip and rolled her eyes. "No, Julian is planning to take Roman to Vegas for his bachelor party, and I was thinking about having my mother actually perform her grandmother duties and watch the kids so we can go."

"Why would I want to go to Vegas for a bachelor weekend?" Nadia asked, looking confused. "Wren, do you want to see Roman get fucked up and make bad decisions?"

"Uh, no not really," Wren replied, looking at Brielle. "You know that Julian isn't going to do nothing stupid on this trip but blow a couple of thousands of dollars."

"You really have to trust that man. Like fully trust him. We...I am not going to be stalking anyone around Vegas," Nadia yawned. "Plus, we have wedding things to do so you're going to be completely occupied."

Brielle rubbed her eyes and huffed. "Why do you hoes always have to talk sense into me?"

"Because if we don't, we'd be in jail and waiting for parole," Nadia chuckled. "Jailhouse orange ain't my color. Speaking of which, I need y'all to spend the night. Please, and thank you."

"You scared?" Wren asked, looking at Nadia yawn and babysit her drink. "Nadia, what is going on with you?"

"Nothing, I just don't want to sleep alone tonight." Nadia shrugged her shoulders and thought about her night with Kwame. She felt safe; she didn't have to wake up in the middle of the night to make sure that her house was still secure. She didn't look over her shoulder once while being with him. There was a blanket of security he wrapped her in, and she was unsure how to take it.

When she did wake up, she smiled softly. She studied his sleeping head on the pillow next to her. Even in his sleep, he still held her tenderly and securely. Kwame's assertiveness was new to her. Part of her wanted to stay in his presence and drop her guard but the other was hellbent on doing things the way she'd always been doing it. On her own.

I don't need anyone's help. I don't need anyone.

She thought to herself to rid herself of the idea of them together. She tried to ignore the aching in her chest that was developing for him. If only she could erase the memory of feeling the wholeness of their bodies. The connection was overwhelming. Nadia has never felt connected to anyone before. This was enough to scare her back inside her shell. She made a conscious decision not to tell anyone what happened between them or what was going on with her. At least not until she could figure it out on her own.

Her phone vibrated across the table, pulling her out of her head. Looking down and seeing Kwame's name, she groaned and answered the phone. "Yeah."

"Yeah?" he questioned, making her thighs clench. Clearing her throat, she looked up to make sure that Brielle and Wren were still having their own conversation. "Don't play with me girl."

"What do you want?" she asked, trying to keep these as normal as she could.

Kwame chuckled and sighed lightly. "You clearly haven't learned your damn lesson. Are you home?"

"Yeah. Everything good with the property?"

"Everything is good. I'll be home tomorrow. When I call back...answer the phone more enthusiastically." Hearing her smack her lips, he laughed. His laugh was a warning, but Nadia tested limits and Kwame pushed back. "I'll see you when I get back."

"I got to go, I got other shit to do than sit on the phone with you," she replied.

"Alright, bet. Remember that baby."

"Mhmm, bye." Hanging up the phone, she ran her hand over her face. "Can I have some more champagne please?"

1 ³ Nadia Garrett

THERE WERE a million things to get done and Nadia was through with L.A. traffic and running around like a mad woman. The only thing she really had on her mind was to stay in bed after Brielle and Wren went home and watch the back of her eyelids. Instead, she was laying on the horn while trying to get Kamaiyah from school.

Wren was showing houses and Roman was in the middle of priming a car. Nadia would do any and every-thing when it came down to Kamaiyah and that's what she had to tell herself while she sat in bumper-to-bumper traffic.

"I swear, I got to move out of Los Angeles," she huffed, resting her head on the tips of her fingers. Her arm was propped up on the armrest of the car and she massaged her scalp, trying to relax her nerves.

While she inhaled in and out, she was interrupted by the ringing of her phone. Cracking an eye open that she recently closed, she scanned to make sure that it was Kwame calling. She'd avoided reading his text and answering his calls like the plague. Nadia hoped that she could avoid him long enough to get rid of the feelings he evoked.

Relieved to see Isabella's name, she still hesitated to answer because of the way Izzy had cursed her and Kwame out for their behavior.

Hitting the button on the screen, Nadia braced herself for what was next. "Hey, Izzy."

"Don't you 'hey Izzy' me," she grunted through the speakers. "I have to find out from Kwame that you flew back early...you couldn't tell me that?"

"I just thought that maybe you were still mad." Nadia bit her lips, being careful not to tell on herself. "You did everything but put your foot up our asses."

Isabella smacked her lips and huffed. "Oh, I wanted to. Y'all made me drink and you know I rarely drink. But you two make my ass itch."

"Well, damn."

"Don't 'well damn' me. You know you need to be nicer to that man," Isabella chuckled lowly. "He talked about your crazy ass all day. That's exactly what he said, your crazy ass."

"Here we go," Nadia huffed and rolled her eyes.

"Don't even act like you don't see him."

Oh, I've seen him. I've felt him. And dammit, I want him again.

"Is that what you called me for? You think you're the matchmaker from Slauson." Nadia shook the visual of Kwame out of her head.

"Because I am the hood matchmaker from Slauson

Avenue. No one has complained about my skills yet, so, get your act together."

"You're a bully."

Isabella's laugh blared out the speakers of the car. "You got some nerve calling me a bully. You are hell, Nadia."

"Alright, Izzy." Nadia closed her eyes and sighed. "Listen, Kwame is..."

She didn't even know how to finish the sentence. All she could do was smile. The battle to fight her feelings was hard. Opening her eyes to see traffic moving again, she found a reason to get out of this conversation.

"Kwame is what?" Isabella asked.

"I'll call you back, Izzy. I'm almost to Kamaiyah."

Agreeing to talk later, they disconnected, and Nadia sighed in relief. She wasn't ready to drop her guard. She didn't care about how much her mind trailed off on Kwame, she wasn't going to give in so easily to him.

Pulling up to Kamaiyah's school fifteen minutes later, she unlocked the door. "Hey."

"Hey," Kamaiyah huffed, getting comfortable in the front seat after putting her seatbelt on. "I graduate in three months. I have to keep telling myself that, so I don't burn this place down."

"Tell me about it." Nadia looked at her and brushed a strain of hair out of her face. "Talk through it."

Pulling off from the curb, Nadia silently waited for Kamaiyah to tell her about her day. "I understand that I am a pregnant teen, but people don't have to make me feel a way about it. I get it. I made this decision but it's my decision. How does my decision affect you?"

"What happened?" Nadia pushed her brows together, tempted to turn back around.

"The dumb ass principle suggested that I consider an

alternative school for the rest of the year because I'm not a good influence..."

Nadia didn't have to hear anymore before she whipped her car around and parked her car in the fire lane. "Come on."

"Nadia...no," Kamaiyah whined as Nadia unbuckled her seatbelt and Kamaiyah's.

"Come on."

Swinging the door open and hopping out the car, Nadia slammed the door and stomped towards the front door of the school. Kamaiyah caught up and trailed Nadia down the hall to the front office.

"Where is the principal?" Nadia asked the receptionist. No, hi, hello, how's your cat and your baby sister's pinkie toe--she was on a mission and there wasn't any need for pleasantries.

"Uh," the receptionist looked up at Nadia oddly, then Kamaiyah. "She's in a meeting."

"In her office?"

"Yes," the receptionist replied. Before she could blink, Nadia was already around the counter and headed towards the principal's office. "You can't go back there."

"Tuh and you're not going to stop her." Kamaiyah shrugged her shoulders and took a seat.

Nadia let herself in the office and looked at the principle and a few teachers surrounding the small table in the corner. "Excuse me, we're in a meeting."

"Not anymore. I'm in a meeting. You can either stay or you can watch. It really doesn't matter to me...did you tell Kamaiyah that she needs to consider alternate schooling because she's pregnant?"

Nadia looked at the principal's face change three shades of red. She sat up and cleared her throat. "Teenage pregnancy is something we don't promote within these walls."

"So, you'd rather get rid of her than help her better herself. You better be happy that she's here and willing to get an education so she can have a leg up. I honestly don't give five kinds of shits what you promote and what you don't promote. She could be anywhere doing anything but instead, she is here, every day on time. Making the grades and running laps around the other students who are probably snorting coke in the bathroom and sucking dick behind the bleachers. That alone should make you proud. Coming where we come from you better be happy she's not striving to be another nigga waiting to jack your white ass at a stoplight," Nadia pointed her finger at the teachers and surveyed the table.

No one budged or dared to talk back to her. "Let this be the last time I have to walk in here and get your ass together. Kamaiyah will be here on time tomorrow, in front of the class. If this becomes a reoccurring problem with anyone else in this school, I will be your worst fucking nightmare. I'm from Oakland don't make me pull up on your ass every day. Y'all have a good day."

Pulling the door closed, Nadia walked toward the exit with a smirk of satisfaction on her face. "Come on let's get some burgers and shakes."

Kamaiyah followed Nadia out of the school and back to the car with a smile on her face. "Thank you."

"Don't mention it. I don't like nonsense."

Nadia pulled off and headed to get them burgers and shakes. Kamaiyah sat across the table from her and munched on her French fries. "Your baby shower is a few months away. Have you given any thought about what you want?"

"Surprise me. I'm not hung up on the details, I just want it to be nice," Nadia watched as Kamaiyah shrugged. "I trust you."

Nadia smiled and took a sip of her drink. "I'm so excited. It's going to be bomb as fuck."

"I know it is."

Finishing their food, Nadia took Kamaiyah home and made sure she was good to go before she left and headed home. Excited to get back in her bed and rest, she rushed home. Parking her car, she grabbed her bag and climbed out. Trudging up the stairs, she fumbled with her keys and looked at her door. It was open. Nadia's senses heightened as she tried not to panic. Backing away from the door, she walked back to her car and started calling Brielle, Wren, Roman, and Julian. No one answered. Her last resort was to call Kwame. What did she have to lose? She was sure that Donte was somewhere around, and she didn't want to take the chance of walking in the house and never coming out.

Hitting his number, he didn't even let the phone ring twice before he picked up. "Now you call me back. I've been calling you all da—"

"Kwame!" Her voice was laced with fear and panic. "I need you. I'm at the house and I was walking in and it was wide open..."

"Get in the car and stay there, I'm on my way."

14

1 ⁴

Kwame Franklin

KWAME TURNED a thirty-minute drive to Nadia's house from his office, to a fifteen-minute drive. He was sure that he would get at least five tickets in the mail from running red lights and cutting people off. Speeding down her street, he pulled up the driveway and hopped out the car. When Nadia saw him rush toward her car, she got out and met him halfway.

"Stay right there," Kwame ordered, and Nadia nodded her head. She glanced at the gun he held to his side while he walked inside of the house.

Sitting on the hood of her car, she chewed on the inside of her cheek while Kwame went into the house like he was the feds. It was ten minutes before he reemerged down the steps. "Nothing looks out of place...who's trying to scare you?"

Nadia looked away, unwilling to tell him that Donte had been snooping around for a while. "Look at me."

Slowly dragging her eyes from her clasped hands to his, she didn't say anything verbally. He read the fear she tried to hide from him. His heart sunk seeing how scared she was while she tried to hold her tough exterior together. "Let's go pack a bag."

Her face twisted and her eye twitched while she processed what he said. Unsure she heard him clearly, she asked. "What?"

"Let's go pack a bag. You're not staying here alone." Kwame wasn't going to rest well unless he knew that she was safe, and the safest place for Nadia to be was with him.

"Where am I staying? With you?" she questioned, furrowing her brow. Kwame balled his mouth up and shut his eyes.

"Dammit! For once just fucking listen to me. Please, go pack a bag," he groaned, taking a step back. Sighing heavily, Nadia slid off the hood of the car and walked inside of the house. Stomping up the stairs to her bedroom, Kwame was right on her trail. He wasn't going to let her out of his sight.

"Don't act like a child, Nadia. Just comply for once in your life," Kwame muttered.

Pulling two duffle bags out the closet, Nadia started packing a few things she needed to get her through what she hoped would just be a day. In the morning, she would have the security company come and change the locks and install extra cameras. She was almost sure, if she had extra security she could go home and be back in her own bubble.

As she packed her things, Kwame looked around the room and nodded his head at her ability to design damn near anything. Her bedroom was warm and welcoming. Inhaling subtle scents of vanilla and lemon, he smirked. He assumed it must've been in her linens because the scent wasn't overwhelming. Placing his hands in his pockets, he moved around the room looking at the pictures she had hung on the walls and placed on the dresser and night-stands; pictures of her and the girls but none of her father, her mother or anyone else. Brielle and Wren were really her family. They all were. Looking over his shoulder as she silently packed her things, his mind raced. He had a million questions to ask her but would wait until she was settled at his house.

"Alright," Nadia spoke up and brushed her hair out of her face. "All packed, happy?"

"Immensely. I love when you listen," he smirked, causing her to roll her eyes.

Kwame pulled himself away from studying the objects in her room and hallway and walked down the stairs behind her. "Don't roll them unless you want them to roll. Feel me? Follow me to the house."

Nadia smacked her lips and dropped her bags on the floor so he could carry them. "You hit it one time and get cocky like it's going to happen again."

"You think it's not?" he chuckled, picking up her bags and watching her walk away. "Ok, baby. Whatever you say."

Carrying her bags down to the car, he put them in the back seat of her car and closed the door. After Nadia locked the door, she walked down the steps to her car. Kwame was standing by the open driver's door, ready to help her in. Instead, Nadia slid in and started the engine. Scoffing softly, he closed the door and walk off to his car. He was going to give her pass for that, they had bigger fish to fry.

Returning to his house, he looked over at Nadia parking her car by his. He could get used to this. But he knew that with her, this would be short-lived. Getting her bags out of her car, he escorted her inside of his house. Looking around the foyer, Nadia whistled.

"If I didn't know any better, I would say you're over-compensating," she spoke up, following him through the house and up the stairs. Kwame's house was definitely a bachelor's pad. It was grand and gorgeous, but it was still missing a touch of warmth. Nadia walked through and kept her hands to herself, not wanting to break anything. Everything looked expensive and like it was on display at a museum.

"You're something else you know that?" He shook his head at her slick mouth. "Make yourself at home."

"Mm," she grunted, looking around. "I'll try...I guess."

He shook his head and opened the door to his room. "I'm not staying in here with you."

"And why not?" he questioned as he dropped her bags in his walk-in closet. "You want to sleep in the guest room?"

"Uh yeah," she replied, folding her arms across her chest. "I don't want to sleep in a bed you shared with other women. I'm cool."

"Other women... okay." Mirroring her body language, he leaned on the frame of the closet door. "What are you afraid of?"

"Nothing," she lied. Surveying the room, she looked over Kwame's dark wooden platform bed, dressed with a plush black and white comforter set. To the right of the bed was the door to the bathroom; from what Nadia could see it was just as big as the bedroom. Artwork hung on his walls and adjacent to the bed was a sitting area that led to the balcony that overlooked the pool. Nadia felt like this was too much house for one person, but it was Kwame. She learned that everything Kwame did and had was big. He had the means to get it, so he did.

"I call bullshit," he grunted, making her refocus from the setup of the room back to him. "What are you afraid of? Talk to me."

"I don't want to talk, Kwame. I just want to sleep...and not with you," she fired back. "Just let me sleep in the guest room."

"Nadia, baby," he groaned, rubbing his temples. "You got to talk to me."

"I'm not your baby," she mumbled, feeling her heart flutter. "Stop calling me that."

"I will never stop calling you that." He looked at her and pushed himself off of the frame. "Answer my question."

"I am not afraid of anything!" she snapped, flailing her arms in the air. She was trying to convince herself that she wasn't afraid. How could she be mortified when she was strong? She dressed herself in armor that no one could get through but underneath that, she was a mess. She couldn't show anyone that part of herself, but Kwame could see it. If he were to tug on her loose thread, she would unravel and be a pile of tangled thread begging to be undone.

He walked towards her and closed the space between them. The closer he got to her, he watched as her shoulders hiked up to her ears and her breath turned shallow. "Yet you called me in a panic. So, it's something. I know you well enough to know..."

"You don't know me," she whispered, refusing to look at him. Stepping away from him, she wrapped her arms tighter around herself. "Just stop it, Kwame. I'm fine, it's nothing."

"No, I'm not going to stop." Hooking her chin in his

fingers, he tilted her chin up and forced her to look at him. "Talk to me. What's going on with you?"

Nadia chewed on the corner of her lip and debated whether or not she was going to open up and tell him everything. It was becoming hard to deny him, especially with him this close and unwilling to back away.

"Donte has been... lurking around for a while now and I've just been trying to avoid him," she released her truth and pulled her face away from his grasp. "I shouldn't have called you. I just freaked out for a minute. I can handle it."

"No offense to your ability to protect yourself, but you can't handle it. You never had a handle on it. I've seen how you look over your shoulder and you jump when someone sneaks up on you. What I don't understand is why you didn't say anything before," he huffed, watching her step away again. Every step she took back, he took one forward.

She wanted to run so bad, but she knew that Kwame wasn't in the mood to be dealing with her shit today. "What was I going to say? Oh, hey, by the way, the guy that violated the fuck out of me is back and won't leave me alone? I'm not going to put my trust in anyone and expect them to protect me. The only person I trust to protect me, is me."

"And that hasn't worked out for you. It won't work out for you if you keep trying to do everything on your own. You scream that you're strong and you got everything under control, but you don't. You operate off of fear, Nadia. How is that any way to live? You don't ask for help but you give, give, and give. Why don't you just let me in so I can lighten that load?" Nadia looked at Kwame and her eyes swelled along with her chest.

Swallowing the hard lump of her truth, she blinked her tears away and looked away. "I don't need anyone, Kwame.

Not even you. People will fail you every time. I don't expect anything from anyone, I never have, and I won't start now."

"You're a liar." He stepped to her and unwrapped her arms from around herself. Placing them around his waist, he wrapped her in his arms. "And that shit sounds great to your own ears but what's the reality of it? Forever alone, looking over your shoulder, pushing people who love you away. Give it up. You got to be exhausted doing this. Shit, I'm tired just from watching you do it."

She was trying to shut down and push him away, but he wasn't going to let it happen. "You are screaming for someone to save you. To listen, to hold you, to show you something different."

She scoffed and tried to break away from him but his hold on her was tight. "And that's supposed to be you? Yeah, okay."

"Man stop denying what you know. Stop trying to fight it." He placed a kiss to her cheek, hoping that it would make her drop her guard just a little. "You can't get rid of me because I'm not going anywhere. I'm going to show you something different. Mark my words. As long as you are with me, you're safe."

He looked into her wide eyes and wiped a lone tear from her cheek. "Please just let me, Nadia. Please."

Nadia sniffled and exhaled. She couldn't bring herself to say anything. It was an effect he had on her. The ability to take her fight. Resting her head on his shoulder, she closed her eyes and sighed. Finally, giving in a little, her shoulders relaxed a little. Kwame placed a kiss to the top of her head while running his hand up and down her back. "I got you. No one is going to bother you."

KWAME LIFTED his head up to see Nadia soundly slept on his shoulder. Smirking softly to himself, he tightened his hold on her, making her scoot closer to him. After he got her to calm down and listen to him, she took a shower and got comfortable. Once she sat down in the sitting area of the room, she started scrolling through her phone and set up an appointment for the security company to come out in the morning. Kwame watched her the other side of the room while getting Amanda to move some of his meetings around so he could tend to her. He took in her silence and her natural beauty that she didn't wear enough. Finding himself in a trance, Kwame took the time to get comfortable. After he showered and changed into a pair of basketball shorts, he traveled down to the kitchen to grab some snacks and a bottle of wine. He knew that she loved her snacks and her wine, and he wanted her as comfortable as possible.

They sat in the sitting area of his room and watched movies for hours. Every once in a while, she would say something but for the most part, she wrapped herself up in a blanket and enjoyed whatever movie was playing on HBO. In the midst of watching the screen, Kwame pulled her body into his chest so he could wrap his arms around her. He was fine with her silence, as long as he could touch her and be in presence, he was content. After a few glasses of wine, she was able to go to sleep without worrying about anything.

Kissing her forehead, he growled to himself at the thought of bashing Donte's head in. His mind flashed back on how terrified she was when she saw him in Oakland and how he poorly handled that moment. He still felt like shit for ignoring all the signs. He was always good and picking up that something was happening with her. Even when she fought and fussed with him. He prided himself of always being her Superman behind the scenes when she only saw him as Clark Kent in public.

Now that he had a better understanding, he would never put her in the position to feel unprotected and disrespected again. He was going to find Donte.

The minute she was gone with Brielle and Wren, he was going to summon Roman and Julian and go handle what he needed to. Until then, he was going to wake up Sleeping Beauty and get her into the bed.

"Baby," he hummed into her ear. He smirked at how she reacted to the word while she stirred in her sleep. Wide awake she opposed it but waking up from a dead sleep, she smiled hearing his voice. "Come on let's get in the bed."

She moaned lightly, sat up and staggered to her feet. Helping her steady herself, he led her over to the bed and pulled the covers back. Climbed into the bed and spreading out, she yawned and drifted back off to sleep. Kwame removed his shirt and crawled into the bed and wrapped his arms around her.

"I got you," he muttered softly in her ear and kissing her pouty lips. "I got you."

She snuggled into his body and hiked her leg over his. With his hand on her back, he watched her lips part and her breathing settle.

You got to show me how to love her correctly. She needs it. Just show me the right way.

1 5

Kwame Franklin

WAKING up in the middle of the night, he reached out to feel her and her side of the bed was cool. Popping up, he was sure that she'd ran away after he fell asleep. Turning the lamp on, he looked around. Spotting her phone on the nightstand, he sat up and started looking for her. He wondered what could've woken her up out her sleep. Opening the bedroom door, he saw a faint light travel up the stairs. Sighing lightly, he walked down the stairs and followed the light into the kitchen. Nadia sat in the barstool with her curls pulled up into a bun. She'd raided his kitchen and found some fruit in the fridge and made herself comfortable while she worked out the final details of Wren's bachelorette weekend and the wedding that was approaching faster than she realized.

Wren and Roman had turned over the full planning of their day, to her. The only thing Wren wanted to concern herself with was the dress and the honeymoon. Everything was booked and moving smoothly, she just needed to finalize their upcoming weekend in Santa Monica. Shifting her eyes from the screen to Kwame entering the kitchen, she examined his bare chest. There wasn't a muscle out of place and his skin was even and chocolate and the longer she stared at him the more she wanted to lick it. Looking back at her screen, she cleared her throat. "I got hungry."

"I thought you ran away," he chuckled lightly, leaning on the other side of the counter. "How long have you been up?"

"A couple of hours," she shrugged her shoulders. "You're snoring woke me up."

"You'll get used to it."

She smiled and shook her head. "You know I don't have any intentions on that happening."

"I know what your intentions are," he smirked and stood upright to walk around the counter. Standing behind her, he put his hands on her shoulders and kissed her neck. "And I have made mine very clear. So, you can throw your intentions away."

Rolling her eyes, she shifted her body on the stool. "Why do you think you can get everything you want?"

Turning her around in the stool, he pushed her legs open and stood between them. Leaning down to kiss her lips, he bit her bottom lip lightly before placing his neck at the base of her neck. They couldn't get enough of each other's lips on each other. It was like that's where they belonged; locked and intertwined with one another.

"Answer my question," Nadia moaned lightly against his lips.

Kwame laughed lowly and sucked her bottom lip. "Because you're everything that I want."

"Quit." She pulled away from him. "Don't tell me what I want to hear. Be real with me. What the hell are we doing?"

"Ending seven years of feuding because we can articulate how we feel," he spoke up, resting his palms on the marble countertop on both sides of her. Resting his forehead on hers, Nadia took her bottom lip between her teeth. She felt a cage of butterflies open up and release in her gut. She never had this feeling for anyone. She was trying to figure out what voodoo he put on her.

"And how do you feel?" she questioned. "Fucking me is one thing. Feeling for me is another thing."

Kwame sighed and tighten his jaw a little. He felt out of control, just like she did. Nadia could be the open flame to his kerosene, or she could be the gentle touch to his rapidly beating heart. "I have been unable to get you out of my head. Long before Scottsdale. You've been the only constant woman in my life. Anyone who has ever asked me to choose them over you has lost. I know you got baggage, but I've been unpacking mine so I can unpack yours."

Her breathing halted and she pulled away to look up at him. His eyes slowly opened, and he nervously traced his bottom lip with the tip of his tongue. Reaching up, she placed her hand on both sides of his face and pulled him back into a kiss. She locked her hands around the back of his neck.

Feeling his nature rise, he pushed her laptop to the side, picked her up and placed her on the counter. Nadia ran her hands down his abs and bit down on her lip. When they got to the top of the basketball shorts, she slipped her hands inside and grabbed ahold on his growing excitement. Rotating her hand around him, she made him groan and back away.

"Come here," he grunted, taking her off the counter and leading her to the couch. Sitting down and letting her straddle his lap, he rested his hands on her hips before taking her lips back into his. Nadia pulled his erected penis out and pulled away from him. Spitting on her hand, she wrapped her hand around him and played with him. She got joy out of watching his eyes get low and he bit on his lip. Vividly remembering how he made her hold on for dear life, she was going to return the favor. It took no time for him to pull her shorts to the side and rub his thumb over her bud. Taking his hand in hers, she locked her fingers around his and slid down on his pole of pleasure.

Kwame groaned and squeezed her hand, feeling her warmth welcome him. Nadia moaned, readjusting to his size before she began to rock her hips against his. She bit down on her lip and let her eyes roll in the back of her head. Her juices covered him, and their lips met again. Kwame reached up, pulling her curls lose so he could grip the root of her har and suck on her neck.

A few minutes of riding slow passed, and she turned it up a notch. Slamming her body down on his, she delighted in his grunts every time she took all of him. Rolling her hips up to the tip and slamming back down, she cursed his name and rested her hands on his shoulders. "Mm, shit."

"Baby...fuck," Kwame grunted, trying to hold on to his manhood and not scream and moan like a little bitch. Holding tightly to her hips, while she wrapped her arms around his neck.

"Don't tap out on me, baby," she moaned seductively in

his ear, tightening her body around him and enjoying her control. Her control was going to cause him to lose his control and he wasn't ready to leave her garden yet.

Wrapping his arms around her, he pushed himself up and laid her on her back. Pulling out to remove his shorts completely and ripping her shorts off. Where they landed, he would worry about later. Pulling her shirt off, he hungrily took her breast in his mouth and suckled each before invading her walls again. Making Nadia gasp, she locked her arms and legs around him as tight as she could. He couldn't lose to her yet. He gave her a little control and realized that Nadia would have him howling to the moon.

Stroking her walls, his husky breathing rested on her neck while she sang her moans in his ear. "Right there."

"You're going to cum for me, baby?" he asked as she arched her back so he could hit her spot. "Mm, leave that shit right there."

"I'm going to cum," she panted with her eyes squeezed shut and her nails digging into his back.

Kwame quickened his pace and bit lightly on her earlobe. "Give me that shit."

Following directions, she released her covering over him and lost control of her moaning. The sweet sounds of her orgasm coaxed his out. His strokes got shorter as he tagged her walls. She was now his, there wasn't any back-stepping. Even if she wanted to run, he wouldn't let her.

Resting in his arms, she still moaned lightly as her body still felt him. Kissing his chest, she rested the palm of her hand on the side of his face. Kwame took her hand in his and kissed her palm. "You messed around and fucked up an appetite."

They'd been laying there for hours--in and out of sleep--

still basking in the afterglow of their session. Still sneaking kisses, still not relinquishing a touch or a glance.

Opening her eyes and looking out the window at the low haze of the sun coming up, she chuckled and sat up. "You should cook."

"I am and then, I'm going to tranquilize your ass. Got me in here about to scream like a bitch." He shook his head and gave her a quick kiss and stood up from the couch.

Nadia smirked and ran her hands through her hair. "You wanted it."

"Yeah, but I didn't know that you had all that shit," he laughed from the kitchen, pulling out pots and pans to make an early morning breakfast for them. "You don't have any actual crazy ass boyfriends I got to worry about?"

"Never had a boyfriend," she shared, searching the floor for her shirt. "Never did commitment."

Kwame looked at her after grabbing everything he needed to make breakfast. "When they said you moved like a nigga, I thought they were joking."

"No joke," she replied. "I just wasn't as loose as you."

Kwame's stoic look made her giggle and shrug her shoulders. "I'm not lying."

"I'm going to break you out that shit. You're not going to be handling me like a little bitch."

Nadia smirked and walked back to the counter and rested her elbows on it. "I'm not?"

"You're not. Why the hell are you smirking? I'm not playing with you. You will not take my heart and run around like you lost your mind."

"I think you've taught me my lesson about mishandling, your royal highness," she scoffed playfully. Kwame smirked and shook his head.

"Part of me tells me you're going to try the fuck out of me."

"Because I am. You should listen to that part," she smiled wide.

"What's it going to take for you to chill out? I got to break your back?"

She shrugged her shoulders. "You can, but I like that shit so that might not work."

"My God," he groaned, whipping eggs in a bowl that he previously cracked open. "You're going to be the death of me."

"Nah, I give you life. Remember that." She pointed her finger before checking her emails. "The security company is going to be at the house at noon."

"Okay..." he replied as though he didn't care. In Kwame's mind, he was ready to move her in. He had her in his grasp, and he didn't want to let it go.

Nadia smacked her lips and rolled her eyes. "I pay entirely too much money for my house, not to be in it."

He grew silent and focused on making her breakfast. She was sure that at any point he would start fussing, but he didn't. After he finished cooking breakfast and plating the food, he handed her a plate. "Okay, we'll go back."

"We?"

"Didn't I tell your hardheaded ass that I wasn't letting you out my sight. Just in case the dumb nigga gets another thought to pop-up, I need to be there."

She licked her lips after taking a bit of food. She was honestly, too tired to fight with him. "Fine."

"Oh, I know it's fine. Eat your food so you can get a few hours of sleep before we go over there."

1 6

Nadia Garrett

NADIA LAID on the couch while Kwame dealt with the security company. She was tired and if he wanted to take control, she was going to let him knock himself out. She flipped through the channels, drifting in and out of sleep. On the verge of falling into a deep slumber, her phone rang making her jump and look around. Groaning, she reached up on the arm of the chair to answer it.

"Hello," she answered tiredly.

"Where are you?" Brielle gritted her teeth through the phone.

"I'm supposed to be somewhere?"

Brielle smacked her teeth. "Nadia, we have the final

dress fitting. Did you forget? I text you last night, but you didn't answer. What the hell is going on?"

"Nothing," Nadia yawned. "I'll be there in a minute."

Groaning, she sat up and pushed her hands through her hair and stood up. She walked up the stairs to change from her sweats and t-shirt to jeans and a t-shirt. Quickly fixing her curls in the mirror, she huffed hoping that she could sleep later tonight. Traveling back downstairs, she found Kwame and told him to lock up if he left.

"Where you going?" he asked, looking over her tired face as she grabbed her keys.

"Messing around with you, I forgot I have a final dress fitting. I need to get there before they get here," she huffed as he smirked.

"Don't want them to know I tagged and bagged that, huh?"

"Nah, it's not that. I would like to finish wrapping my head around this before I get them involved with my business," she shared as he nodded his head. "I'll see you later."

Walking away, he cleared his throat. "You forgot something."

"What?"

"Get over here and kiss your nigga, girl."

"My nigga?" She rose her brow and dragged herself back to him. Kissing him quickly, he held her tight and planted a kiss that would leave her thinking about him while she was away.

"Your nigga, get used to it." He released her and smiled. "Be safe."

"I will," she chuckled as he smacked her ass as she turned and walked out the door.

Speeding to get to downtown, Nadia checked the rearview mirror to make sure there wasn't any evidence of

Kwame on her skin. Brielle and Wren were going to find out one way or another. She preferred to tell them when she was ready than have them sniff it out.

Arriving at the boutique, she sashayed inside and spotted Brielle and Wren looking over the dresses in the full-length mirror. Joining the group, Wren looked at her with a raised brow.

"I'm sorry. I was up all night working and completely forgot," Nadia shared, hugging both of them.

"So, that's a no to grabbing food after this. You look like you need to sleep for days," Brielle pointed out, making Nadia squint her eyes at her.

"Well, I can't sleep for days because we leave for Santa Monica in two days. But sleep is definitely on my list before I go and lose my mind with you," Nadia informed the group. Any unnecessary details, she purposely left out.

Turning her attention to Wren standing in her simple wedding gown, she smiled. "You look so pretty. I cannot wait."

"I cannot wait..." Wren smiled, "until all of this die down, and I can just enjoy my man. Y'all don't be mad when I turn my phone off and disappear for a while."

"I won't, Brielle maybe because you know she needs attention. Go live your life girl." Nadia grabbed her dress and got to try it on. Walking back out to join the girls, Brielle and Wren raised their brows.

"Your ass is definitely bigger than last time," Wren examined her and narrowed her eyes.

"Why are you looking at me like that? Every time we're together we drink and eat. What did you think was going to happen?" Nadia asked, looking at her ass in the dress. "And it's always been big."

"Mm," Wren pressed her lips together, making Nadia

smack her lips. "If a plane crashes, I know who is going first."

Brielle bust out laughing and shook her head. "Nadia has enough to keep us full for a very long time."

"I should've stayed home," Nadia teased.

"Then I would've shown up to chop you in the throat," Wren warned.

"I'm gonna have to back away from the table or my ass is going to bust out the seams," she huffed to cover her smile. If she kept messing around with Kwame, she was going to have to actually work out.

Wren giggled and stepped down and gave Nadia a side eye before stepping close to her. "Why are you so happy?"

Nadia raised her brow and stepped down. "I can't be happy to be around you?"

"Bitch, you're never this happy. I'll figure it out." Wren gave her a once over before Brielle could join them.

"The only thing you need to figure out is your playlist so I can give it to the DJ, miss thang," Nadia smacked her lips, following the three of them to the back to get out their dresses.

"Thank you for joining us. We're going to meet at my house and go from there." Brielle was so happy to have a weekend away from her kids. It was comical the way she clapped her hands and bounced from side to side.

"She's been talking about this trip for weeks," Wren giggled. "Nadia is there anything you need for it?"

"Ask me that again and I knock your teeth out. I told you I had it. It's paid in full...everything. You don't need to do anything but get drunk and enjoy yourself," Nadia spoke up before walking to the cashier to give them the final payment for her dress.

"Well, I just wanted to make sure. You're not even

charging me for the wedding," Wren groaned, following her to the cashier.

"Can you let us just take care of you and relax," Brielle rolled her eyes.

"Fine," Wren hummed, studying Nadia lowly. She sensed that something was different, and she was going to figure it out. "I'll see y'all Friday."

After handling their business, they hugged and went their separate ways. Nadia headed home just as fast as she traveled to get to the boutique. Her bed was calling, and she couldn't wait to answer it.

Walking into the house, she looked around at the cameras. Dropping her purse and keys on the table by the door, she kicked her shoes off and yawned. Walking through the kitchen, she spotted take out containers on the counter and information left from the security company. Too tired to eat or read, she walked into the living room to see Kwame knocked out on the couch. He was curled up on his side snoring while the TV watched him. Laughing softly, she moved his arms and snuggled by him. Automatically, he wrapped his arms around her and kissed her forehead.

Instead of letting her mind run a million miles a minute, she inhaled his scent off his shirt and drifted off to sleep.

NADIA HAD her outfits spread across her floor and packed her bag for a weekend of fun away with the girls. Kwame was downstairs on the phone handling business, leaving her in her own world. She couldn't believe that the man that irritated her soul for the longest was now the one comforting it.

Her smile hadn't faded, even when she fought for it to.

She'd been exposed to another part of him. Underneath the sarcastic asshole was a man that wanted to be loved and give love. He didn't ask for much, having her in his arms was enough for him. Being that Nadia never really had a relationship, she could get used to this. She still was cautious in exposing her entire heart to him. In the event he dropped it, it wouldn't be too hard to move on.

Finishing her packing, she put her suitcase by the door and climbed in the bed and turned on the TV. Surprisingly, she hadn't heard from Donte since he attempted to break in. She didn't doubt that he hadn't been snooping around but Kwame had made his presence known. Donte was too much a coward to fight a man. Instead, he terrorized her when there was no one around to do anything about it.

"Don't go down to Santa Monica and lose your mind," Kwame entered the room, pulling her out her thoughts.

Rolling her eyes, she smacked her lips and watched as he climbed into the bed by her. "I'm grown and I do what I want."

"Yeah, okay," he replied, putting his phone down on the nightstand. "You got everything you need? I hope you're not wearing that bikini you had on in Catalina."

"I sure will be wearing it," she commented with a smirk, enjoying the sight of his face twist.

"Nadia," he groaned.

"Kwame," she returned, raising her brow. "I'm wearing it, don't even try to fight me on it. You won't win."

He smirked slyly and turned to look at her. "You should model it for me."

"I don't think so. First of all, I have to be up early tomorrow and will not be up all night and second of all, none of my panties or pants or shorts have survived you."

"You haven't figured out yet that you shouldn't be wearing them, then I don't know what to tell you."

Nadia rolled her eyes. "But you be tearing up my good shit."

"I'll buy you more, but I'm only going to tear them up."

She dropped her hands in her lap and shook her head. "Well, you spend money like water anyway so restocking my La Perla and Simone Perele ain't an issue for you, is it?"

"Ain't no need for you to wear them if you're with me, baby. I want it when I want it," he smirked.

"Boy shut up," she groaned and rolled her eyes.

"So, you're really not going to let me see it again?"

"No, if you weren't getting head in the foyer you could've seen it."

"Boy, you lie like a rug. You would've still kicked me out." Kwame smacked his lips and rolled his eyes.

"You're right," Nadia laughed. "But you could've watched my booty while I did it."

"You be with the shits all the time. Don't worry, I'll see it. That's not even a problem."

"You are annoying." She settled into the pillows and smiled at him.

"You like that shit."

"Mmm, the jury is still out. Find a movie so I can go to sleep."

Kwame frowned his face and looked at how comfortable she was getting. "Are your hands broken?"

"They don't work. You're the one who said you wanted to lighten my load, so lighten my load and find a movie. Babe."

1 ⁷

Wren Franklin

THE RIDE to Santa Monica was quiet for the most part. Nadia never slept on her way anywhere, but she was knocked out with her mouth open. Wren looked over at Brielle and nudged her. Bringing her head out of her phone, Brielle looked over at Nadia passed out.

"Something is going on," Wren whispered.

Brielle smacked her lips and went back to pecking away on her phone. "Sure is, Julian called the babysitter."

"For what?" Wren questioned. "Aren't the three of them supposed to watching two sleeping babies?"

"That's what they said," Brielle groaned. "I swear it's always something with that man."

Wren paused and looked at Brielle. "Why are you all of

sudden not trusting him? What has happened? Every moment he has, he's at home with you three. You have the codes to his personal and his work phone. What the hell could he be hiding."

"I don't know but it's something."

"I think you're tripping. I think you need to relax and accept that your husband has learned his lessons. If he's getting a babysitter it means that three of them are collectively up to something and when they are normally together and up to something, someone is getting their face beat in," Wren shrugged, pulling her phone out to send Roman a text.

What are y'all doing?

Kwame needs us to ride with him...nothing big

...Tell me about it when I get back

Bet...

"Well whatever Kwame is up to, I'm sure it will not lead Julian down the path of destruction, so relax. This entire weekend you need to put that phone down and drink and enjoy your girls...or me at least because she has been really tired lately," Wren replied, chewing her lip. "Bri, I'm telling you there's something that we don't know."

"Girl," Brielle rolled her eyes. "Fighting every day gets tiring. You know the minute we get there she's going to be wide awake and bossing us around like she does."

"Don't I know it, she has a schedule," Wren giggled, watching Nadia stir a little.

"First of all, hoes," Nadia grumbled, picking her head up off the window and wiping her face. "Y'all are loud. I am not bossy all the time and I am drained."

"Mm," Wren pressed her lips together. "Can you please tell me what's going on with you?"

Nadia looked over her friends and smiled. She wanted to tell them, but she wasn't going to take away the attention from Wren on her weekend. "I am finding happy. And part of that happiness is to sleep. And eat. And repeat."

"Nadia who taught you how to lie?" Brielle asked, looking up from her phone.

"You did." Nadia smiled and pulled her phone out excited for something from Kwame but nothing. Putting it away, she focused on enjoying this weekend with Brielle and Wren.

"You did, though," Wren laughed. "You taught us all how to lie."

Kwame Franklin

"You mind telling us where we're going?" Roman asked, watching Kwame slouch down in his seat while gripping the stirring wheel.

"I've asked him that ten times already. He ain't gonna tell us. We just got to ride with the Dark Knight where the bat signal leads him," Julian mumbled, replying to Brielle's million and one text messages. "Listen, this better be worth it. Brielle is tearing my ass up through text."

"Blacky Chan has on leather gloves and he checked his clip before he cranked up. I got a feeling we are going to beat someone's ass. I just need to know why," Roman chuckled from the back seat.

"Nah," Julian spoke up. "If he tells us, we can't testify

for him. It's better to say nothing until we get back to the house."

"You right. You might be kind of smart Big Bird."

"I might be?" Julian asked. "I run an entire ER unit."

"You know out of the string of dumb shit you've done. I've come to realize that you have a brain up there. Congratulations."

Julian rolled his eyes at Roman and glanced over at Kwame. He was locked into whatever he was about to do. None of the guys asked why they were riding but they needed to ride. No one ever rode by themselves; when they needed each other, they were standing there waiting on the word.

Finally reaching their destination, he put the car in park and put the gun in his waistband. There were parked in the parking lot of a janky motel. "Who the hell is staying here?"

Julian curled his lip up in disgust while Kwame got out the car. Following suit, Roman and Julian followed Kwame through the parking lot and up the stairs. "The better question is why did we drive the nice car," Roman muttered.

Kwame had done an excellent job of ignoring both of them. For the last two days, he'd been tracking down Donte's whereabouts. Nadia had been content and safe with him and he wanted to keep it that way. It all came down to one final conclusion, Donte had to go.

Julian and Roman strolled behind Kwame, looking over their shoulders to make sure no one was going to roll up on them. Stopping at the door, Kwame pounded his fist against it until it was answered.

Donte pulled the door open and looked at Kwame, Julian, and Roman oddly before realizing who they were. Julian and Roman were just as surprised as he was. "Y'all them niggas that be rolling around with Nadia...fuck you want?"

Kwame stood there silently for a couple of seconds just to look over him with a curl of the lip and twitch of the eye. Donte smirked and Kwame reached out and grabbed him by the collar and pushed him back into the room. Following them in the room, Julian and Roman shut the door behind them and stood by waiting, in case Kwame needed their assistance. But from the looks of it, he seemed to have it all under control. Donte may have had height on Kwame, but he lacked in strength because Kwame was slinging him around the room like a rag doll.

Fists to the face, body shots, and bashing his head into any and everything he could. Roman knew that Kwame claimed that Crenshaw raised him, but he didn't know Kwame had all of this in him. It made him wonder for a moment what triggered this aggression.

Donte tried to fight back but there wasn't any use. Kwame had the upper hand and had he put his hands on him, Kwame would have killed him and gotten away with it. Sprawled over the floor, Donte groaned trying to stand to his feet.

Kwame kicked him back down and pressed his foot in his chest. "You call her, I'll fuck you up, you show up to her house, you threaten her peace in any way, I will make sure I kick the life out your lungs. Are we clear?"

Donte attempted to answer but Kwame repeatedly stomped on his chest before Roman and Julian pulled him away. "He ain't worth it man."

"Keep your bum ass away from her, bitch."

Julian pushed Kwame to the door as Roman scanned the room to make sure they hadn't left anything behind in the tussle. Following them to the car, Julian forced Kwame into the passenger seat while he climbed into the driver's seat. Cranking up the car, they sped off and headed back to Julian's house.

Once Julian parked the car in the driveway, Roman said what he'd been dying to say since they pulled up on Donte. "Y'all fucking!"

"I swear I thought the same thing too," Julian spoke up. "You beat that nigga like he stole something from you. Since when do you start fighting Nadia's battles?"

Kwame removed his gloves and got out the car. Leaning on the hood, he looked at Julian and Roman propped up on different parts of the car. "You gonna tell us when this started?"

"No," Kwame replied.

"Nigga, don't play. You and Nadia have been at each other's throats for years and magically y'all a thing?" Julian asked. "Give us the real shit, nigga. What's good?"

"Y'all are over thinking this shit. He's been popping up and making her life a little difficult, so I just did what I've always done," Kwame shrugged his shoulders.

"Be Superman to Lois Lane," Julian nodded. "I can't be mad at that, that's some honorable shit. Just don't play the back too long. You want that shit, you got to get that shit."

"One hundred," Roman spoke up. "Tag and bag it before our couple's trip."

"Yeah," Kwame nodded, standing up. "Let's go finish playing daddy daycare before Brielle comes back from Santa Monica and kicks Julian's head off."

"You ain't lying about that," Julian scoffed. "She's been on some crazy shit lately."

"Probably because you knocked her ass up," Roman spoke up.

"Why you always wishing babies on people?" Kwame

asked, looking at him as they walked in the house like nothing happened.

"Because that's one thing Julian can do right. Make a baby," Roman laughed.

Kwame shook his head and plopped down on the couch. "That's true though."

"Would both of y'all shut up," Julian groaned as the sitter walked downstairs to give him the rundown of the night.

Kwame pulled his phone out his pocket and debated whether or not to check in with Nadia. He missed her. Holding her. Inhaling her scent. Feeling her warmth on his body. He missed her.

It was clear that in the process of trying to break Nadia down and get to her heart, she broke him down in the process and stole his. He wasn't even sure that she knew that she did. Kwame always knew that he would get her, but he didn't think that when he got her, he wouldn't see his life without her.

It could've been a mixture of her drug that he was still high on, or it could've been that after years of fighting each other he wanted nothing more than to fight with her, while they fought for each other. He'd taken a stake out on her heart and no matter what it took to claim it, he was going to come in and take everything that was owed to him.

At the top of that list was Nadia. He was intentional in his motive and how he felt. It took years of heartbreak, self-reflection, and aggravation to see everything he needed was right in front of him. He wanted nothing more than shower her in love.

One thing Kwame took away from Terry in his old age was, when you loved a woman correctly, and you showed her that a man's touch wasn't supposed to be painful, she flourished. Nadia was already a rose with thorns but he was excited to see how she bloomed under the proper love and care he could provide.

Putting his phone away, he decided to let her enjoy herself and when she returned home, he would show her how much he missed her instead of telling her. Nadia needed action, she had enough words and broken promises to last her a lifetime.

His actions were going to prove differently, and the love that grew inside of him for her was going to forever change her and him for the better.

1 8

Nadia Garrett

PULLING her bags into the door, she was hit with the aroma of food. Parking her suitcase by the door, she closed the door and walked into the kitchen to see Kwame in the kitchen creating a feast. She was looking forward to seeing him, but she figured that he disappeared on her. She was actually expecting him to create some sort of excuse to why he couldn't be with her or why this wouldn't work out with them.

"Hey," she smiled, traveling further into the kitchen. Looking over his shoulder, he smiled down at her. Turning around fully, he wiped his hands off on the towel and wrapped his arms around her before kissing her lips tenderly.

"I thought you forgot about me," she whispered against his lips. "Got me all worked up to drop me like a bad habit."

"Mm, nah. Not yet," he teased, making her roll her eyes. "I wanted you to enjoy yourself and helping Julian with the babies was a handful."

"I bet it was. I would have paid to see that."

"Nah, it was a mess. Go get comfortable. I'll be done soon."

Breaking away from him, Nadia went upstairs and walked into her room. Her eyes were automatically drawn to the bed where a bouquet of flowers was tied together with a pink ribbon. By the flowers were a silk robe, teddy, and a note.

"Shower, get dressed, and meet me downstairs for dinner and dessert," she read aloud. "He's so nasty..."

After showering and oiling her body down, she looked in the mirror and pulled her curls out of her bun. Any chance he had to put his fingers through her hair, he did. Since her clips got snatched out, she hadn't thought about putting them back in. Giving one final glance and an approving nod to herself, she walked downstairs and caught Kwame pouring her a glass of wine to go with dinner.

She smiled and looked at him before tilting her head to the side. "You do know that you have to keep all of this up. Because I'm going to be spoiled and expecting it."

"I know. Lucky for you, I like that smile on your face so it's light work. You smell good."

"I always smell good," Nadia replied, sitting down at the table. She watched him scoff before putting her plate on the table. "Terry taught you how to cook?"

"He did. That and my mom worked all the time, so I had to eat somehow and I'm not going to eat out all the time. I'm frugal...sometimes," he spoke up after kissing her cheek and sitting across the table from her. "You know you have to cook for me."

"Where's that in the rule book?" Nadia took a sip of her wine and rose her brow.

Kwame chuckled softly and looked at her. "There isn't a rule book, we're winging this shit and figuring it out as we go. Which means you got dinner tomorrow."

Nadia smirked and nodded her head. "Fat Burger it is."

"Don't even play with me girl," he chuckled. "Eat up, you're going to need that energy."

Clamping down on her lip, she narrowed her eyes at him and bit into her salmon Florentine. It was second nature to defy everything he said because she'd been doing so for so long. She already figured out what would happen when she tested his limits, although she couldn't walk straight for a few days, she would try him again.

Kwame had her figured out. In order to keep Nadia from constantly trying him, he was going to shower her with all the love and attention she faked like she didn't need. By the time Nadia got her footing and wrapped her head around everything, it was going to be too late to get out the fortress of love he built around her.

She thought that dinner was satisfying as she laid on her stomach in the middle of the bed with her head rested on her folded arms. Kwame's oiled hands glided up and down her thighs. Every so often he would kiss every exposed part of her skin. He would glide his hands up to her center, stopping before he could touch it. He did this enough to make her flower throb with anticipation. He wasn't ready to take her yet.

Feeling him massage her body made her moan lightly. His strong hands ran up her thighs, over her ass, and up her back to her shoulders. His body hovered over hers and he could feel her anticipation. Kwame prided himself on making each time better than the last. Tonight, he didn't want to neglect an inch of her body.

Her teddy was hiked up over her shoulders and her robe laid at the end of the bed. Kwame was still dressed, but the minute Nadia was able to get her hands on him, he would be out them in a minute. "Turn over."

Lifting her head and turning over to see him over her, she propped herself up on her elbows and watched as he balled his hands into a fist and ran them along her legs and the sides of her body. He had her legs propped on both sides of him. After a while, she was sick of him teasing her. Her excitement was trickling down her thigh.

Kwame removed her teddy and ran his hands over her breasts, up her shoulders, and around her neck. Nadia took this opportunity to sit up fully and push him off the bed. "It's my turn."

"It's not about me though." he watched as she stood up and took the oil off the nightstand.

"Well it is now," she took control. Pouring the oil in her hand, she placed the bottle back down and ran her hands together. "Take it all off."

"All of it?"

"All of it. Your ears not working?"

"Keep it up," he grumbled, warning her about her mouth.

Nadia smirked and bit her lip. Watching him undress and hold her gaze was going to make her cum without even feeling him. "I plan on it."

Kwame flexed his muscles while he stood in front of her bare body. Nadia reached out to rub his chest, his arms, his back, his firm ass, and his legs. "Don't get carried away girl."

Nadia laughed and squatted down as she ran her hands

over his legs. His massage was going to end with a happy ending because well, she wanted it too. "Turn around."

"That's it?" he asked, looking down at Nadia in the squatted position and smiling up at him. "Oh...do your thing baby."

"If you stop trying to be so damn bossy and let me do what I'm doing," she muttered, pulling him closer to him so she could take him fully into her mouth. Kwame's groan was music. Nadia began to suck, slurp, bob, weave and swallow every ounce of him that she could. One hand to cradle his balls.

Running her tongue along his length, she jerked him off while sucking on his balls and returning back to his pulsating rod. "Damn, girl."

She was bringing him to the edge. Her hair was a mess from his hands being unable to grip anything else. Without warning, he released himself down her throat. Nadia moaned while swallowing him whole. She didn't stop sucking him until he was fully erect again, and he pulled himself away.

In one swift move, he picked her up from the squatted position up to the bed. Hooking his arm around her waist, he pulled her close enough to her only to leave enough space to enter her. Once he was deep inside, he rested his weight on his elbows. "Tell me how you want it," his husky voice was in her ear, making her wetter than she was.

The sound their bodies made when they became one was music to him. The more he talked to her, the closer he was to confessing his feelings and being sure to leave a piece of himself inside of her while she slept.

Nadia locked eyes with him and rotated her hips around him slowly. She was drenched in pleasure. "Baby, I missed you."

Automatically she flooded again. There was no rush to reach their peak. Every stroke was purposeful and sensual. "Mm, baby," she moaned, holding on to him. The pride in his chest swelled.

Noses touching, eyes locked, eruption after eruption, affirmations of never letting go or running away were exchanged. When they finished, the sheets would need to be changed, showers would need to be taken. They didn't see the end, they just continued to hold on to each other and enjoy the euphoria they exchanged.

Laying on her chest, he listened to her heartbeat. "You don't have to worry about Donte anymore."

Nadia opened her eyes and looked down at his bare body resting on hers. "What are you talking about?"

"I took care of it," Kwame simply answered with a shrug and a kiss to the breasts. "We had a conversation."

"I doubt you verbally talked to him. I am sure your fists did most of the talking. You didn't have to do that," she spoke up, reverting into the role as her own protector.

Kwame lifted his head up and looked at her wide amber eyes. "Why wouldn't I protect you?"

"Because..." she started and then paused. "Because I was going to take care of it. I didn't need you to protect me."

Kwame chuckled, shook his head and sat up completely. "Nadia, baby. I have always protected you. I have always made sure that nothing interfered with your peace. I started seven years ago, and I won't stop now. You can drop your guard. I'm not going to hurt you, and I damn sure not going to let anyone else do it either."

Nadia's eyes grew wide while listening to Kwame tell his truth. She watched as he stood up and walked into the bathroom and press his palms on the sink. Laying there a little longer, she let the information he gave her sink in and marinate. He loved her, he always had. He just wasn't ready to love her until now.

Sitting up, she looked at his back covered in fresh scratches. "What do you mean you've always protected me?"

"Exactly what I said," he huffed. Her initial response irritated him a little but then he quickly understood why she responded the way she did. Protection from anyone but herself, terrified her. Turning around to look at her now sitting on the edge of the bed with her feet dangling off, he sighed. "Since the day I met you, I had this overwhelming uncontrollable need to protect you. I knew I couldn't love you then, but I knew I could protect you at the least. So, I did. I never stopped. That weekend in Oakland, I beat myself up for not picking up on the threat he posed sooner. But I made sure that he would never think about bothering you."

Nadia looked at him. Examining his posture, she chewed her lip and tried to think about when he had time to live his life and protect her. Kwame crossed his arms across his chest and watched her watch him. "Vinny..."

"Vinny?" Nadia squinted her eyes and tilted her head to the side, thinking about the last encounter she had with him that extended past the night where he ditched her. "You're the guy...wait...what?"

Her mind was spinning trying to wrap around the extent of Kwame's reach. "I saw him the next day after the party and he told me I was better off with the nigga that would fight for me because he wasn't it. You fought him...for me...after I blew you off?"

Kwame nodded slowly and cleared his throat. "I did, and I will always do it. I hated how he treated you that night. You have always deserved better. After you stormed off from the party, I followed you back to your dorm just to make sure you got there okay. I went back to the party, but it sucked because I just wanted to spend the night with you, but I knew eventually our time would be here."

Nadia's eyes filled with tears. She couldn't control her emotion. She tried to fight the tears and sobs escaping but she couldn't. She covered her mouth and shook her head. She was in complete disbelief. Moving from the bathroom back to the bed, Kwame pulled her in his arms. "I'm sorry. I had no idea."

"You don't have shit to be sorry for," he assured in her ear and kissed the top of her head.

"No one has ever protected me, I wanted them to but no one did. I had to do it on my own. And I'm tired of fighting. I'm tired of living in fear. I'm tired of having to work extra hard to show everyone I'm tough and I got this all under control. I'm tired." Before she could wipe her tears, he did.

"Then stop. I got it from here. I can fight for both of us. I will show you that a man's hands aren't supposed to hurt. All I ask for is you in return. Every piece, withholding nothing. Just ride, don't change shit."

Nadia rested her head on his chest and wrapped her arms around his waist. "Thank you."

"Ain't no need to thank me. Your heart and your bomb ass loving are enough, baby. You don't have to change for me. I know who you are and how you are, and that shit does it for me. Okay?"

"Okay." She kissed his chest and pulled away from him. "We have to change the sheets. When I say we I mean you because I'm going to shower to forget I broke down like a bitch."

Kwame laughed, watching her walk into the bathroom.

"You just going to leave me out here to do all the hard work."

"You can choose to do hard work in here with me or change the sheets." She shrugged her shoulders and turned the shower on.

"Both."

1 9

Nadia Garrett

THEY WERE WORN OUT. After a session in the shower, they finally got around to changing the sheets and going to sleep. Nadia didn't give a second thought holding him close and admiring him. She was hard but around him, she could be soft enough. She didn't have to wear her armor. She didn't need to wear makeup or the extensions to feel like she was that bitch. She was that bitch because now she could take her armor off and be vulnerable in the walls of her castle.

Kwame laid in the bed perfectly content with Nadia, scrolling through her phone and selecting things that she needed for the Scottsdale location. They didn't need to talk their presence was enough. Her leg rested over his and her hand was behind her head and his head rested on her chest. Her heartbeat was melodic, and it was going to lure him back to sleep.

"I got to make this cake for tomorrow," she groaned, dropping her phone in her lap. "It's already two o'clock."

"Shit," Kwame groaned while sitting up, allowing her to move before laying back on the pillows. "You know at some point you have to actually sleep."

"I will, just not right now. Or tomorrow," she huffed. "When I made these plans, I didn't take into account that maybe I would stop hating you and want to ride your face all night."

"First of all girl," Kwame kissed his teeth and rolled his eyes. "Hate is a strong work. You were really feeling me. Tell the truth and stop fronting."

Nadia curled her lip and scoffed. "Kwame...you are so full of yourself it's nauseating."

"You talk shit like I won't have you screaming and begging for me to fill you up," he smirked.

"You are nasty."

"And you aren't? You bit my ass last night."

"No, I didn't."

"Oh, yeah that was definitely you."

Hitting him with the pillow, Nadia laughed. She swung her legs over the bed and shuffled down the stairs to start making the cake for Kamaiyah's baby shower. Grabbing a few pillows, he rolled over and went back to sleep.

Reaching the kitchen, she propped her phone up on the back of the counter and started taking out everything she needed to start the process of making this cake. Once she got the cake whipped up and poured into individual pans, she placed them in the oven and went to lay on the couch.

A nap was needed. She hadn't had this much sex in her whole life. She couldn't complain; it was good, intentional loving. Whatever crack Kwame was serving her almost made her lose all her sense. Getting stupid on him wasn't on her list of things to do but she would continue to appreciate the small things he did.

Looking back on all their encounters, she could now pick up on the things that drove her crazy but she should've known it was his inability to come out with his truth.

Dozing off to the thought of Kwame Franklin, she was woken up by a ringing phone and a blaring timer. Groaning, she sat up and huffed. Answering Wren's FaceTime and traveling into the kitchen to take the pans out of the oven, she smiled faintly. "Hey!"

Looking at the screen to see both Brielle and Wren wave, she returned the gesture. "We were just eating and talking about you. Figured we would just call. It looks like we woke you up."

"You did, but it's all good," Nadia, sighed propping the phone up and beginning to make the icing for the cake. "I've slept most the day anyway."

"Are you depressed? You've been sleeping a lot, you don't come out anymore unless you have to," Wren spoke up, looking at Nadia's tired eyes and her wide smile. "Not to mention you haven't gone to the salon to get your hair blown out."

"First of all, I am not depressed. Second of all, what's wrong with my hair?" Nadia couldn't wipe the smile from her face. It was time to tell them. She was confident that Kwame wasn't going to run away, and she knew that she wasn't going anywhere. She just needed to give him a hard time every now and then.

She could feel Kwame's presence approach her. Kissing her cheek, he walked to the fridge to grab a bottle of water. "Bitch, who was that?" Brielle asked, snatching the phone from Wren's hands to get a better look.

Nadia laughed as she watched the screen shake and rotate before they steadied it. Kwame wrapped his arms around her shoulders, smiled and waved at his sister and Brielle. "Biiitttttccchhhhhhh!!!"

Wren damn near screamed and Brielle pretended to pass out. "What the hell? When did this happen! Both of y'all be holding out."

"I needed to make sure it was a thing before I told you. I wasn't initially trying to hide. I wanted to be one hundred percent sure," Nadia announced in a giggle fit at their reaction. "I hate y'all. Y'all are so damn dramatic it's ridiculous."

"I can't believe what I'm seeing." Wren looked at the screen with tender eyes. "Y'all look so good together."

Kwame smiled like a kid in the candy store. "You see that Lil Bit. Tagged and bagged that ass! That's me right there. Ain't no running."

"Seriously, would you quit?" Nadia groaned as Kwame rested his chin on her shoulder and ran his hands over her hips, making her shift. "Stop it."

"Thank God!" Brielle flailed her arms up in the air. "Kwame can you let her come up for air so we can talk about you? Like tonight. Like in two hours?"

"Damn, she's going to have to go if that's the case." he nodded and stepped out the view of the camera.

Nadia watched as he pushed the stool back and pushed her shirt up over her hips.

"You two are ridiculous. I still cannot believe what I'm seeing. So, our set up in Catalina helped?" Wren asked as Nadia tried to maintain her composure as

Kwame spread her legs open and pulled her folds into his mouth.

"Uhh no," Nadia struggled to talk normally, feeling her body flood underneath his control. "Come over for dinner, I got to go."

She hung up as fast as she could to focus on Kwame. Pushing her hips closer to his face and holding on the sides of the stool, Nadia rotated her hips on his face. She was going to overdose on him if she wasn't careful. "Ah shit."

Kwame smacked his lips, enjoying the taste of his woman. Making her quake under his control, he held her tight while she climaxed over him and the stool. When he finished and stood up to kiss her lips, she shook her head. "Why are you so nasty?"

He enjoyed the scent of her love on his lips. He also wanted her to anticipate what was going to happen when he got back home to her.

"The same reason you like it," he replied, smacking her thighs. "I'm going to get up with the guys before Brielle and Wren get here. I know y'all got gossip to catch up on."

"You do know that you are going to be the gossip, right?" Nadia informed, standing up and to clean up their mess. "You're going to be the highlight of the night."

"Because I'm that nigga. I got you to bend over and give into a nigga. Easy."

"Easy? The only reason that happened is because you got checked." Nadia smacked her hips and rolled her eyes. "Uh, back that shit up. I got you to bend over and give in to me. You're the one chasing me around with your nose wide open."

"Girl, don't even front."

"Boy," she rebutted, looking at him with her hands on her hips. Kwame turned around and walked back to her.

She backed up and pointed the spray bottle at him. "Stop it. You know what's going to happen if you come over here. There's going to be cake and frosting all over the kitchen. You got to be tired, I know you're tired."

"Mmm, nah. I got a sweet tooth like a fat kid." He turned away and smirked on his way out the kitchen. "I'm a grown ass man, you know that shit, act like it."

"I'm a grown ass woman who has you moaning her name on command," Nadia replied, watching him freeze and look over his shoulder at her smug smirk.

"What did you say?"

"I believe you heard me."

"You better remember that shit when I get back. We'll see who's going to be moaning what."

"Yeah, you moaning my full name like I'm the man, baby."

Kwame started climbing the stairs and shook his head with a smirk. "You talk shit for a living."

☙❧

Nadia had wine chilled and dinner cooked by the time the girls arrived. Her curls were wild, and she had a glow that could shine freely now that the secret was out in the open. She sat on the couch with a glass of wine, looking at Brielle and Wren look at her.

"Bitch if you don't tell me how this happened. From the beginning and don't spare the details. I'm trying to understand how you two went from damn near killing each other, to not being able to not keep your hands off each other," Brielle sat on the floor next to Wren, looking up at Nadia like it was story time in kindergarten.

Nadia sucked in a deep breath and looked at them. "Okay, so boom...Catalina, he showed up with a hoe, I kicked them out, but you know Kwame. He came back and everything was cool, like calm. We didn't fight, it was like we were actually friends and I was comfortable. It was weird and uncomfortable that I was comfortable, but I didn't want to pull away. Part of me kept nagging me to run. We vibed and all that and I lost my mind for a second and we kissed but you know me. I don't do that feelings shit, so I left."

Wren cut her eyes are her and shook her head. "You're the worst."

"Anyway after that, I avoided him like the plague until we got to Scottsdale and argued all day about whatever. I was trying to walk away from him, and he grabbed my arm. My instinct was to slap him, and I did..." Nadia continued her version of events and Wren cut her off.

"Oh, he hates that shit. I know you got your ass torn up." Wren shook her head.

Nadia bit her lip and chuckled. "I did. But even then, I shrugged it off. It wasn't until Donte broke in..."

"Excuse me what?" Brielle and Wren questioned at the same time.

"When the hell were you planning on telling us that?" Brielle fussed.

"Honestly, I wasn't," Nadia shrugged her shoulders and pushed her hair out of her face. "I wasn't going to tell anyone. I was going to handle it myself and keep pushing. But he wouldn't let me go. So here we are...together. I've never been in a relationship, but it feels right, I guess."

"You guess?" Wren hollered. "You are glowing...it's all over you."

"It really is," Brielle smiled, pushing herself up from the

floor and sitting by Nadia. "You deserve this. Take every-thing he gives you."

"Please," Wren chimed in. "He loves hard, so I know you're going to be taken care of. You should know some-thing though."

"What?" Nadia asked, placing her wine glass down.

"Terry told him to knock you up."

20

2°

Kwame Franklin

WALKING INTO THE CIGAR SHOP, Kwame sat across the table from Julian and Roman and tossed both of them a stack of money. Looking at him oddly and then each other, Roman and Julian shrugged their shoulders while Kwame ordered his drink and cigar.

"Y'all won," he spoke up after the waitress walked away. "Y'all got it. She got my ass. I never thought I'd see the day that I wanted to wake up to her every day."

"I knew it," Roman waived his finger at Kwame. "I knew you were bullshitting the other night. How long have you been hiding this from us? I thought we were boys. I thought we were better than secrets."

"Shut up," Julian chuckled. "Nah but seriously..."

"Not long. We just wanted to wrap our minds around it," Kwame answered their question followed by a shrug of the shoulders.

"So my question is, how are you going to keep this going? I have never known Nadia to be in a relationship. She does what she wants, she says what she wants...she ain't no damn joke. She makes me nervous as hell," Julian admitted. "She will kill you in your sleep and not flinch."

"She ain't that— okay she might be but there is no plan to keep it going. Just keep it going. Showing her something different is all I'm trying to do. There is nothing that she can do to make me leave or fall back. You spend years fighting with someone, you learn what makes them tick and who they react to when you trigger them."

Roman kissed his teeth and cut his eyes over to Julian. "You see this shit?"

"Mmhmm," Julian hummed into his glass. "You a smooth motherfucka."

"And it's annoying."

Kwame laughed and rolled his eyes. "I tried teaching y'all, but no one wanted to learn from the master."

"It don't matter now," Roman laughed. "We all in love and shit. That's crazy as hell. I didn't think Julian was going to make it..."

"Nigga," Julian kissed his teeth and cut his eyes at Roman. "When are you going to stop riding my dick..."

"Pause!" Roman pushed his seat away from Julian. "You're going to just say that all loud with these people in here. They're going to think you're my type! You are way too light for me."

"Whoa who said, love?" Kwame questioned, looking at Julian and Roman who looked at him like he was tripping. "I didn't say that."

"You don't have to say that shit. We see it. Own that shit," Julian spoke up, ignoring Roman. "If you love her, you love her. That's it."

"But please don't tell her that," Roman shook his head quickly. "I don't know how to take a non-hostile Nadia."

"Nah, I'm not planning on it. She's still hostile, I don't see that ever changing and she still got her running shoes on. I can see that shit in her eyes. I'm not saying anything that's going to make her think she can get away from me. I mean, I've always loved her mean ass, this is just a different level. I'm new to this shit," Kwame released as the waitress returned with his cigar and drink.

"Do you need me to light that for you?" she asked with a seductive smirk. Kwame didn't even look up at her. Roman and Julian watched intently to see if Kwame was going to give in.

Kwame picked up the cigar and clipped the end and shook his head. "No, I got it. Thank you."

She lingered around longer than she needed to, and Julian looked up at her. "He has a girlfriend that fights for fun...she'll snap you in half like a twig, that's after she slaps you in the teeth. I've seen it."

Kwame chuckled and nodded his head. "This is nothing but facts. She'll fight me too. Not the life I want to live, and I like my teeth."

That was enough to get the waitress to frown and walk away. "Julian, I got a grand that says he's going to be engaged by the end of the year."

"I say at least by the time we go to the lake for our vacation." Julian nodded his head.

Kwame pushed his brows together and curled his lip. "Why are y'all betting on my freedom?"

"Freedom?" Roman questioned in his outside voice.

"Nigga you don't want your freedom. You want Nadia. You chose your outcome already. This guy said freedom."

Roman and Julian laughed and exchanged their unintelligible banter while Kwame lit up his cigar and shook his head.

"Remind me to never tell y'all shit else."

༄

It had officially been two weeks since Kwame and Nadia's relationship was out and talked about. Now that it was, he had to report the news to Terry before Wren did. Because he took the advice from the old man, he knew he would have to come back and give him his props.

Walking into Terry's house, Kwame found him busy in the kitchen whipping up dinner before Farrah returned home from work. "What's up Pops?"

Terry retired years ago, and he prided himself that when Farrah walked in from a long day she had a meal waiting on her. It was the small things that Kwame picked up from his father that outweighed the big things he had to get over.

"Hey, what's going on? You and Wren been too busy to come and see me? That's messed up," Terry teased, looking up at Kwame. "You look happy."

"You are too old to be in your feelings like this," Kwame chuckled lightly and leaned on the counter. "I hope you're making enough for us."

"Us? You seeing people because ain't nobody here for you," Terry continued to tease.

Rolling his eyes, he looked at Terry and smiled. "Nadia had to handle some final wedding stuff for Lil Bit, but she'll be here soon."

"Nadia huh?" Terry stopped what he was doing to look at his son and smile. "You tagged and bagged it?"

"Tagged and bagged, all me."

"How you feel?"

"Me?" Kwame smiled his million-dollar smile. "I feel good. I'm happy, she makes me happy. Who would have thought?"

"I knew it. I saw that hate all in her eyes. Farrah used to look at me like that too." Terry nodded his head and smiled at his son. "I'm proud of you son for stepping up to the plate. But I told you, all you had to do was tame her."

"Pops," Kwame laughed. "You met the same woman, right? Ain't no taming her completely and I don't want to. I can calm her ass down a little bit, but I don't want her to be anything but herself."

"That's big shit son. You talking like there's no end in sight."

"There isn't. You said when you know, you know. I'm not going to ask her to marry me today. But I know that's what I want. But before that, I got something else I need to secure for her." He stood up straight and put his hands in his pocket. "My company is dissolving soon. I get to keep all the clients I've acquired, one being Isabella. I want to keep that business separate from the rest, so I'm thinking about handing it over to Nadia. She has the hang of it, she's a beast when it comes to staying on budget and making that shit shake."

"Then get your paperwork in order and take care of your queen. One thing that is automatic is that if you take care of her, she will always take care of you. It's give and take. And for a woman who swore up and down that she was going to be alone for the rest of her life, she might not say it but she's depending on you. She's going to give you her heart and expect you to handle it with care," Terry shared, returning to his cooking. "Be the man I should've shown you. The man that I know you can be, and everything will fall where it's supposed to."

"Thanks, Pops," Kwame smiled, dapping him. "This shit is crazy to me though."

"Anytime. It's not every day my son walks in here with his chest puffed up, talking about he tagged and bagged it. Especially not with a young lady, I like. You know she's been my daughter since she walked through the door the first time Wren brought her over," Terry laughed. "Dammit y'all fought like gang members. Don't ever lose that feeling though."

"I remember that. Her damn mouth is slick. But I like that shit." His smile didn't fade an ounce.

The front door open and laughing took over the house. Farrah and Nadia walked into the kitchen side-by-side, laughing about whatever it was they were talking about before walking into the house. "Hey, Kwame."

Farrah greeted him with a hug and kiss to the cheek before moving around the counter to kiss Terry. Nadia followed suit, kissing Kwame and going to hit Terry, who wiped his hands off so he could hug her tightly. "What are you two in here doing?"

"I was cooking, and Kwame was..." Terry nudged Farrah and pointed to Nadia and Kwame engulfed in one another. "I knew it. I knew that one day that y'all would stop fighting."

Terry looked down at Farrah and kissed the top of her head. "Reminds me of us."

"I really didn't like you though. But those Franklin men and their charm."

"I just threatened to knock his head off his shoulders

this morning." Nadia shrugged with a smile before pulling away. "The only reason he's standing is because of that bottomless charm. Otherwise..."

"But I fixed it didn't I?" Kwame spoke up. "Didn't I?"

"You did," Nadia bit her lip lightly. Terry watched how they interacted with each other and couldn't help but smile proudly. His son was happy. He couldn't have asked for anything more than that. Even though the path they both took to get here was long, drawn out and full of confusion and unspoken emotions. They were here now, basking in the light of the sun.

2 1

Nadia Garrett

WITH HER HANDS in her lap, she looked around the room the way she did every session. Yvette was used to Nadia's avoidance of the topic of her mother, but this was the last barrier she had to break through. Yvette was accustomed to Nadia's way of operating. Just because she let you in one door, didn't mean that there wasn't another trap door behind it. It was years of unpacked damage and trauma she had to face in order to fully move on and live a happy life.

Yvette laughed softly and sat back in her seat and looked at Nadia. "You always do this. We spend thirty minutes staring before you get to the point you want to talk about the topic. Did you get the Donte situation figured out?"

Nadia sucked in air and looked at Yvette. "That situation was handled for me...by my boyfriend...I have a boyfriend..."

Nadia said it out loud, still trying to get used to the way it sounded coming off of her lips. "I am in a relationship with a man I have fought and ran from since the day I met him..."

"How did you end up in a relationship with someone you couldn't stand?" Yvette was curious. She placed her notebook and her pen down. "Especially after warding off love. I'm interested."

"A mixture of things," Nadia smiled and lifted her head. "Intruding friends, therapy, and realizing that he was the only one to get any type of emotion out of me. The more I think about it the more I realize that I kept him at arm's length with any and everything is because he scared me. His affection is so much. I'm not used to that."

"Why do you think that is?"

Nadia licked her dry lips and exhaled. "No one has ever given me affection or taught me affection. For years all I had was me to love me, to teach me, to make sure I was safe and okay, you know? I got used to that. I settled with that idea of forever lonely. But every day he shows me something new about myself and what it's like to care for someone."

"So, you see yourself with him for the long run?" Yvette asked, crossing her arms on her lap.

Nadia chuckled lightly in disbelief and let the smile cross her face as she nodded her head. "Yeah, I do."

"How are you going to start something new with him if you haven't dealt with your pain in its entirety? Yes, things are beautiful right now. But what happens when they aren't? When life happens and something he does, or something he says triggers you to revert back into the part of your life you locked behind a door, so no one can see it?" Yvette's comment made Nadia's smile fade as she locked eyes with her. "What are you going to do then? Runaway and leave two hearts broken. You have to talk to your mother. You have to finalize that transaction and check out for you and your wellbeing. I can see that happiness all over you. Don't let that toxicity you buried take over your garden."

Nadia huffed and looked away. She dreaded the idea of going back to Oakland, but she knew she had to do it.

"Nadia, if love is really what you want, and love with him is what your heart is pushing you to, then you need to go back to Oakland and close that door."

"I know," she spoke softly, filling her lungs with air and releasing it. "I know."

"Call me after, call me during if you need me. I'm rooting for you to win. You're far too good of a woman to have that be the reason you set limits to how hard and vast you could love yourself or someone else."

Wrapping up their session, Nadia hugged Yvette and headed home. She kicked her shoes off and sighed. She didn't want to go to Oakland, she wanted to say she did. The thought of going consumed her so much that didn't even hear Kwame come in. Nadia managed to cook dinner and almost drink half a bottle of wine by herself while she thought about all the possible outcomes of this trip that needed to happen sooner than later.

Feeling Kwame's hand on her back and his lips on her cheek, she pulled away from him. She didn't even look up at him. He twisted his face and looked down at her in deep thought. "What's going on?"

Nadia shrugged her shoulders and shook her head. "It's nothing."

"It's nothing?" Kwame asked. He could clearly see it

was something and he wasn't taking that answer. He was not going to let her shut down after getting her to open up. He looked at the half empty bottle of wine and shook his head. "It doesn't look like nothing."

Leaning on the counter, he watched her look at everything but him. "Am I going to have to pull it out of you?"

"No, because I don't want to talk about it. I don't want to think about it, but I can't stop," she groaned and sat the glass down before catching his glare.

"Tell me."

She chewed on the inside of her cheek before sighing and rubbing her forehead. "I went to therapy today...I'm in therapy by the way. Might've left that detail out. Anyway, we talked about you for a bit and she asked me how could I start something new with you and not handle my past."

Kwame chose not to say anything at all. Listening to her was more powerful than anything he could tell her. "She's been pushing me to go back home and see my mother."

"When are we going?" Kwame asked, looking at Nadia push her brows together. "Oh, you thought you were going alone?"

Kwame laughed and stood up. "You know better, baby. We got the wedding in a few days, then the trip so we should go soon and get it out the way."

"Are you sure?" Nadia finally spoke up, looking at Kwame nod his head. "You don't have to come with me."

"Stop that," he stood up. "Let's leave in the morning. I'll book our flight now. It's going to be fine alright?"

"Alright," Nadia nodded her head.

"Get over here and kiss me like you're supposed to," Kwame smirked and opened his arms to receive her. She pulled herself from her position and walked into his arms. Kissing his lips, she stepped back. "I see you cooked."

"Yeah, I was actually trying to think. So, there's that."
She was still consumed with the fear of going home
tomorrow.

Gently rubbing her shoulders, he kissed her cheek.
"Everything is going to be okay."

"I hope so."

THE NEXT MORNING, they were in the air on their way to
Oakland. Kwame was sure to be completely patient with
her. He knew that this trip was going to cause her to feel
things that she'd put off for a long time. The only thing he
wanted to do was to make sure that she felt supported.

After arriving in Oakland, the first stop on their journey
was her father's gravesite. Only visiting it for the second
time, she was still heavy. Squatting down in front of his
tombstone, she huffed and wiped the dirt from the top.

"I see you've been left unattended," she mumbled to the
stone and shook the dirt off her hands. "I didn't get to tell
him bye, she just let him go without seeing me."

Kwame stood by her as she stared at her father's name
etched in the stone. "I always wondered if he asked for me.
He wasn't the best father, but he was mine you know. He
loved me; I knew that. As far as everything else he fell
short, but I knew he loved me. I was his baby girl.
Princess."

"So, he's responsible for you being a brat?" Kwame
asked as Nadia stood up and placed her hands on her hips.
Smiling, she shook her head.

"He is. At least in the aspect of me holding myself to a
certain standard," she shared and placed her hand on top of
the tombstone.

"If you could tell him one last thing what would it be?" Kwame asked, placing a hand on her shoulder.

Her lip quivered but she didn't let her tear escape. "I would tell him...I love him. And I carry him with me every day and everywhere I go. And that I'm sorry for being mad at him for so long. He didn't know...I didn't tell him."

She took a deep breath and hummed as she released it. "Mmm. That's all I would say...we can go now."

"You sure?" He didn't want her rushing through this or any of the feelings that were coming to the surface. "We can stay if we need to."

"No, I'm good. Let's go see her and get this over with," she sighed before walking away.

The ride to her mother's house was the longest ride she ever took. Kwame held her hand in his and squeezed every now and then to silently remind her that everything would be okay. When the car pulled up in front of her childhood home, she dropped her head and did a few breathing exercises before getting out and walking up to the front door.

Knocking lightly on the screen door, she stepped back feeling Kwame's hand on her lower back. She appreciated him being there. She didn't know what could possibly happen when she walked inside. She silently prayed that her mother wasn't home. The minute she finished her prayer, the door opened.

Pat looked surprised to see Nadia standing on her steps. She frantically pulled the door open and unlocked the screen door. "Nadia..." her voice broke as she took her only child into her arms and held her tightly.

Nadia cleared her throat and pulled away. "Hey, ma."

"Come on in." Pat stepped out the way, letting two of them into the house. Nadia looked around and a wave of emotion took over her. "I didn't know you were coming. I didn't think you were coming back here. You brought a friend..."

"I'm Kwame," he smiled and outstretched his hand. "Nadia's boyfriend."

He noticed that she'd grown completely silent. Like being in this space took her voice away. Now he knew why she was so vocal. She didn't have a voice when she was here. She was unheard. To him, her silence was louder than she could ever be. "I've never known her to have a boyfriend."

"Because I never did," Nadia mumbled. "He's actually the reason I'm here."

She walked over to the couch and sat down on the edge of it. "Since the last time I saw you... I decided it was time to fix me and go to therapy."

Pat and Kwame both sat down and looked at her. "It's been a year of self-reflecting and acknowledging what hurt me and why it hurt me. I don't want to live the rest of my life afraid..."

Pat pinned her brows together. "I've apologized to you, Nadia. How many times do you want me to do it?"

"Got damn, mom. Can I finish my thought?" Nadia snapped. There were the emotions she was afraid of. Even Kwame jumped a little hearing Nadia's voice flip like a switch. "For once let me talk...please. You know what...I don't care you don't have to. Don't apologize. You don't even know how to take ownership of your shit. Everything is everyone else's fault. You had to work harder because daddy gambled and drank. You couldn't watch me, you couldn't love me. The list is extensive, and I am so fucking tired of letting that be the reason I stifle myself. The truth is, I hate you. I have hated you. For everything..."

Nadia's tears were spilling over, her voice was broken, and she was on the verge of sobbing. Kwame tried to take her hands, but she yanked away from him. "I can't do this shit!"

Nadia sprang to her feet and stormed down the hall to the bathroom before she completely broke down. She couldn't close the door fully before she started sobbing uncontrollably. Her hand pressed against her knees as she cried like a baby. Kwame eased into the bathroom and pulled her into his arms. The sobbing made her weak. She leaned on his body for support as she cried.

He let a few more moment pass before he stepped back and held her face. "Look at me."

Looking at her with a face covered in tears and snot, he wiped her face. "Breathe."

She tried and started crying all over again. He shook his head and held her face tighter, stepping into her and pressing his forehead against her like he was trying to take her pain away. "Breathe."

Inhaling deeply, she started to breathe and calm down. "Tell her what you have to say...once you get it out, how she takes it is on her. It's not your burden to carry anymore. You can lay that cross down after you get everything out. Understand me?"

"Yeah," she whispered. "I'm –"

"Don't you even dare say sorry. I got you. You hear me?" He pulled away and looked at her. "You hear me?"

"Yeah. I hear you."

He kissed her forehead and let her go. "Go ahead and say what you got to say, baby."

Nadia returned to the living room and sat down and looked down at the worn-out carpet and sighed heavily. Pat was still seated with silent tears streaming down her face. "All I wanted you to do, mom, was protect me. You didn't and it's fine now. There's nothing you can do to take it back or even stop it from happening. I've been so angry for so long and I am tired. I am so tired of letting fear and anger run my life because I worry about someone hurting me. I am thirty years old and this is my first relationship. The first man who I am not petrified of. The first man who makes me want to love him with whatever part of my brokenness that I can. This is the first time in my life I thought about becoming someone's mother. Funny thing is I was planning on getting my tubes tied at the end of the year because I feared becoming someone's mother and failing them."

Kwame stood in the hall and listened to her put everything on the table. Pat sniffled silently and listened to her daughter. For the first time, she was listening. "Everyday, I wake up and I want to be better. I actually think that I am capable of loving someone and I know that they will love me back. You taught me a very valuable lesson that I will hold on to for the rest of my life. You can forgive after the people God put in place to raise you and protect you, fail. I forgive you. Not for you by any means. But for me. I deserve better. That man in the hall deserves better. And that's what I'm going to give him. I hope and I pray that you can forgive yourself, too. Everything had to happen for me to be who I am now. I would have never found my voice if it was never stolen from me."

Nadia released the rest of the air from her lungs and wiped the remainder of tears from her eyes. Looking at Kwame, leaning on the wall, she nodded her head. "I'm ready to go home."

Nadia stood to her feet and put her hand on her mother's shoulder before kissing her cheek. "Thank you."

With that, she walked out of the house with Kwame behind her. She climbed into the car and sat quietly as they headed back to the airport. Nadia didn't say anything until she laid in the bed next to Kwame. Turning her head to face him, she placed her hand on his cheek. "Thank you. I mean that with everything. Thank you, you didn't have to, and you did."

"Don't thank me. That's my job."

Nadia smirked softly and kissed his lips. "Now that you've seen where I come from...behave on this trip to Vegas, so I never have to tap in to my Oakland roots."

Kwame laughed and kissed her back. "You can't go a whole day without shit?"

Nadia laid her head on his chest and threw her arm and leg over him. "No, I can't."

"You don't have nothing to worry about. Don't even think about it. Plus, Julian got to walk a tight line. I might blow some bread but that's about it."

Closing her eyes, she inhaled the scent of his flesh and felt like a load of weight was lifted off of her shoulders. She managed to come to terms that her destiny was now in her hands, and she didn't have to move forward in fear.

"So, that appointment you made to get your tubes tied," Kwame spoke up after silence fell between them.

Feeling his hand rub down her back, she yawned and held on to him tighter. "I canceled it last week. I don't want to do it anymore. I have the possibility of a future and I'm going to hold on to that."

Kwame smiled and closed his eyes. Holding her close to him, he relaxed and drifted off to sleep.

2^2

Nadia Garrett

Nadia looked at Julian, Roman, and Kwame with her eye twitching and her lips pressed together. They were all hungover, in fact, Kwame held his head and propped himself up on the wall while Roman groaned, laying on the couch in the men's suite.

"Are y'all serious? The wedding is in an hour and you're still hungover?" she questioned. "No one was responsible enough to say, hmm maybe we shouldn't be doing this?"

"No," Julian groaned. "We only drunk more thinking that we would be okay."

Nadia curled her lip and shook her head at their collective stupidity. "You three are too old to be so damn stupid."

"Please stop yelling," Kwame damn near begged.

"Oh, I haven't even begun to yell yet." She turned on her heels and stomped out the room, letting the door slam behind her on purpose. Going to dig into her bag, she found a bottle of Advil and some sodas from Isabella, who was setting up the reception on the other side of the building. Returning back to the group of idiots, she handed them two Advil gel capsules a piece and a mini bottle of coke. "Take these and be dressed in thirty minutes. Roman wake up! I will start this on time. Y'all better pull it together."

Leaving out for the final time, she fixed her face before she stepped in the bridal suite to see Wren in full breakdown. "Kamaiyah what happened?"

"She's been like this for ten minutes, I've tried to calm her down and she won't stop crying," Kamaiyah replied, in almost the same panic that Wren had. Nadia groaned and dropped her head back before rushing to Wren's aid.

"Kamaiyah, could you go find Brielle?" Nadia asked Kamaiyah, who nodded her head and scurried out. Nadia hiked up the bottom of her dress and sat on the floor with Wren, who had cried so much in ten minutes she ruined her makeup.

Taking a handkerchief, Nadia wiped her face and rubbed her back. "Roman loves you. He really does. You're crying over nothing. He's not leaving, he's not going to find someone else, he wants you and no one else. He wants you to fight with him and push him to high standards. That's all he wants. You're crying for nothing. Your makeup is running for nothing. You're too far to turn around. Where are you going to go? To Henry Taylor?"

"Oh, hell no," Wren sighed, settling her crying. "Never ever again."

"Then wipe your face, stand up and let's get married.

When this is over, we can drink and dance the night away. Okay?"

Wren looked up and nodded her head. Nadia stood to her feet and reached out for Wren to take her hands and stand up. Balancing on her feet, Wren wrapped her arms around Nadia and hugged her. "Thank you."

"Don't thank me," Nadia hummed. "I love you. It's your day, I am not going to let you talk yourself out of the best thing to ever happen to you. I know you're nervous."

"Is he here?" Wren asked as Nadia nodded. "He's good?"

"He is," Nadia smiled. "He's here and getting ready to rock and roll. He'll be up there waiting on you. Now please sit down, drink some champagne and get your make up touched up."

The door of the bridal suite opened, and Brielle and the makeup artist walked back in. "Is she okay?"

"Now she is," Nadia sighed and sat down as the makeup artists swarmed around her. "You know Wren."

"I stepped out for ten minutes to check on the kids," Brielle sighed and shook head. "Well, you know that she's the emotional one. I knew it was coming."

"Y'all know I can hear you hoes," Wren spoke up as the make artist put a cool towel on her face to shrink her puffy eyes before retouching her make up.

"So?" Brielle asked. "In here crying for nothing."

"Bri." Nadia shook her head and laughed. "Stop it."

"Ignore her, she's mad at me," Wren spoke up.

"Mm," Brielle pressed her lips together and rolled her eyes. "She forgot her dress, I turned around to get that. She forgot her shoes, I turned back around. You know I turned around five times because she remembered some-thing every time. Not like we didn't pack her stuff last night."

"Brielle you were like this at your first wedding," Nadia laughed. "We all were actually. Leave that girl alone. By tonight she will be drunk grinding on her husband and in two weeks we'll be in the lake picking on her again."

"Brielle needs to worry about her speech and leave me alone," Wren huffed.

"I got my speech ready to go. Don't worry about me."

Nadia shook her head at the back and forth of Brielle and Wren. She was so happy for Wren. She was happy for all of them, it seemed like everything was turning out better than she could've ever imagined.

Stepping out the room, she made sure all the final details were handled before going to check on the guys. They were looking better than they did, seeing Roman stand up was a relief to her. It was one thing for Wren to be crying about her nerves and another for her to meet her groom at the altar, barely holding on.

Standing in the hall with her arms folded, she felt someone stand by her. Looking over to see Terry, she smiled. "Hey Pops."

"Hey daughter," he chuckled. "You've done such an amazing job."

"No, need to thank me. I would do it a million times over for Wren," Nadia said with a shrug.

"I know you would. A little birdie told me you were doing this for free," he chuckled softly and handed her an envelope. "Here's a little something for all your hard work. Don't tell anyone I gave that to you. But I want you to use it for your dream. Whatever that may be. I watched you pour into everyone else; I want to pour back into you. You're my daughter whether you came from me or not. I want the best for you."

Nadia felt her eyes cradle tears as she threw her arms around her neck. "I want you to know you'll always have a father in me."

"Thank you so much. Between you and your son, you two are making me soft." Pulling away, she wiped her face and smiled while taking the envelope from his hands.

"There isn't anything wrong with that," Terry nodded and smiled seeing Kwame appear in the hall. "Make sure you same me a dance tonight okay?"

"I will," she smiled after kissing his cheek. Wiping her face, she looked at Kwame walk over to her. "Feeling better?"

"I'm holding on, you're going to take care of me?" he asked, putting his hands on her hips. "I think I just got better, seeing you in this dress."

"Even with a hangover you're nasty," Nadia shook her head and rolled her eyes.

"All the time for you and I missed you."

"Good. I'll figure out if I'm going to nurse you back to health after I get your water bucket of a sister married. Go get the guys, it's show time." Kissing him quickly, she broke away and walked away leaving him there to adjust himself and round up the crew.

The room was full of people from both of their families, even Ronnie showed up to see Roman take another step in his life towards greatness. Since his dinner with George, Roman had been a lot more active in his old neighborhood. He and Ronnie had grown closer and Roman even started showing him a better way of life than the one he was used to.

Their friends watched proudly from the aisle as Wren

floated down with a huge smile plastered across her face. Her arm was wrapped around Terry's. His expression mirrored hers as he whispered something in her ear that made her giggle. Once they reached the foot of the altar, Terry handed his daughter over to Roman with a smile on his face. Before taking Wren's hand, Roman stepped down and hugged Terry. The wedding party could see both of them tear up before they let go.

"I got you," Roman nodded. "I'll do right by her."

Terry stepped back and let the officiant take over the ceremony. Brielle dapped the tears from her eyes and Nadia blinked hers away. She made sure she looked at everything but Kwame. If she connected eyes with him, she was going to lose it.

Roman and Wren's exchange of vows was tearful, honest, and beautiful. Nadia smiled on, elated that they finally got it together. She didn't know what the future held for her and Kwame, but she was hopeful. For the first time in ages, the thought of tomorrow didn't frighten her. She knew that with Kwame by her side she would be okay. Her heart would be protected, and his intentions would always be pure towards her. Because of that, she found herself falling. Guards were dropping and her heart swelled in admiration and respect for him.

After the wedding ceremony, guest flooded into the reception to eat, drink and celebrate the new union. The reception started off with a party. Three dances in, everyone helped themselves to whatever they needed. The entire room was happy and lively. Brielle, Nadia, and Wren danced in a circle with one another with drinks in their hands. Well, Brielle was nursing a club soda, but Nadia wasn't going to blow up her spot. She was just going to enjoy the night.

Love on Top by Beyoncé blared through the speakers and the girls had their old routine memorized down to a T. Julian, Roman and Kwame looked at how happy they were.

"You're next," Roman nudged Kwame, who threw his hand up in the way.

"I don't know why he's frontin'," Julian laughed, taking a shot of Hennessy and handing one over the guys. "Drink that shit."

"So, we're going to be hungover two days in a row?" Kwame asked. "Alright, this Henn gonna have my baby fucked up."

"Spare me the details," Julian chuckled. "Just do your thing dawg."

"Bow wow," Kwame smirked, focusing on the trio shake their asses. Taking a shot, they all looked at each other. "Time to break this shit up."

Moving from the bar to the dance floor, Kwame wrapped his hand around Nadia's waist letting her grind against him. These were the moments they lived for. All six of them with a smile plastered across their faces enjoying each other and the lives they built. This was what it should have always been like. Smiles, cheers, inside jokes and love.

Kwame silently made a declaration to himself that they would stay like this. From this moment forward, anything that threatened the peace of this circle and his family wouldn't stand a chance. This was his haven and he would fight for it to stay intact with every fiber of his being.

2 ³

Kwame Franklin

Two weeks had passed since the wedding. Roman and Wren were out of the country until next week. Brielle and Nadia were out shopping and get everything ready for the trip to the lake. Kwame figured while the girls were busy, him and Julian could catch up without Roman's ridiculousness.

Down the street from Kwame's office was a jewelry shop. Popping in for a minute, he browsed the watches and waited for Julian to show up. From the watches to the earrings and necklaces, he ended up at the engagement rings. The impulse grew stronger since Roman tied the knot with Wren. Waking up to Nadia wasn't making it any better.

Kwame could no longer hide that he indeed loved her, and he couldn't shake the idea of her being his and only his. They already wasted seven years being enemies, he didn't want to waste any more time waiting for the right time to make her his wife. What was the point?

"Do you see something you like?" The jeweler had been keeping her eyes on him just in case he needed help. "Are you looking for a special lady or just looking."

"She's been a pain in my ass for seven years," he mumbled, leaning over the glass with his hands in his pockets. "Let me see the one on the end."

Kwame pointed to a 14-carat halo cushion cut ring. Nadia wasn't flashy but he wanted a ring that would stop men in their tracks and turn around and stay clear of her. He couldn't be around her every second of the day, but his stamp could.

Nodding her head, the jeweler pulled the ring out the case and handed it over to him. "It's the only one like that. It's my favorite."

"It's dope," he nodded his head and looked at it. "I feel crazy as hell."

"Love does that to you," she informed as Julian walked in. Getting closer to him, Julian stopped and leaned on the counter.

"You're really doing it?" Julian smirked as Kwame studied the ring. "This is some wild shit. The player has put his game down so he can marry the only woman who will talk back to him."

"And check my ass and make me better." Kwame took in air and exhaled. "I was sure I was never going to get to this point with her. Breaking her down is hard as hell."

"You just got to let that shit happen," Julian coached. "She's let her guard down a lot for you. Just take that shit.

Give her real love, not what you think she needs but what she really needs."

"Thanks, bro." Kwame nodded his head and handed the ring back to the jeweler. "I'll take that one."

He dug in his pocket and pulled his wallet out. Handing his card over, he palmed his face and nodded in acceptance that he was leaving his past in the past and moving forward.

"When are you going to do it?"

"Probably at the lake and get that shit out the way. At this point what am I waiting for?"

"I thought you would've wanted to wait until you're old and gray like Terry, but I see you learned a good lesson from your pops," Julian chuckled and looked at his phone. "Every time Brielle swipes the card, my banking app sends me an alert. All I know is there better be something for me in all this shit she's buying."

Kwame laughed and shook his head. "I probably will never have this problem. Getting Nadia to share the blanket is hard enough. Sharing money is out the window. Is Brielle going back to work?"

"Nah, she already made it very clear that as long as we have kids she's not going back," Julian replied, locking his phone and sliding it back in his pocket. "After we remarried, she told me that trying to have it all isn't worth not having anything."

"I got to say, I am happy as hell that everything worked out for y'all. I don't ever want to go through that shit." He didn't even want to think about Nadia breaking his heart or worse, breaking hers.

Julian looked over at Kwame and sighed. "Man, listen. As long as you two are on the same page and always meet in the middle on everything you'll be fine.

Don't psych yourself out. Don't go into the expectations of what it's like because your expectations will fail you every single time. Just hold on, don't let go and enjoy the ride. That's what I learned, that's what I keep learning."

After signing the receipt for the ring, Kwame thanked the jeweler and headed out with Julian. They made plans to meet up at Julian's house and travel to Big Bear Lake.

After this weekend nothing in his life would be the same, but it was another chapter that he was excited to embark on.

☙❦❧

EVERYONE SAT AROUND THE FIRE, laughing and drinking. Roman and Wren were wrapped in each other's arms, Brielle and Julian couldn't keep their hands off of each other and Nadia sat on the couch with her back resting on Kwame's chest.

Shot glasses were spread across the table and everyone but Brielle were on the verge of being completely drunk. Wren suggested playing two truths and a lie while they watched the sunset over the lake.

"Alright," Brielle spoke up. "It's my turn, I guess. I'm going back to work, I slashed my professor's tires once, and I'm pregnant."

Wren and Nadia looked at each other before looking at Brielle. "Well, I know for a fact that you slashed you professor's tires..."

Wren shook her head in laughter. "I remember that night."

"How much shit did y'all do in college?" Roman asked, looking at the three of them. "Slashing tires, making cakes in peoples gas tanks, flirting with the professors to turn in an assignment at the end of the semester."

"Roman, that's not even everything. That's light work." Nadia shook her head. "You're definitely not going back to work so you're pregnant...you're pregnant."

"Oh my God!" Wren screamed shot up with Nadia right behind her. "I'm so happy for you!"

Wren and Nadia stepped over Roman and Julian like they were invisible and wrapped their arms around Brielle. "I knew it. I've been watching you nurse that soda all night and take water shots. This is amazing!"

Brielle and Julian smiled from ear to ear. Roman and Kwame congratulated Julian with half hugs and cheers. "Tagged and bagged," Julian chuckled, nudging Kwame to make his move. "Do your shit bro."

"Alright that's enough," Julian spoke up. "Give me why wife back, you two can scream and jump in circles later."

"So rude," Wren huffed before she let go of Brielle and returned to her seat.

Nadia took her set by Kwame and tucked her legs under her. "I'm saying, he could've let us finish our celebration."

"No, because we never finish a game. Something happens in the middle of it and y'all get all distracted. It's Kwame's turn anyway," Julian scoffed lightly, prepping the moment for Kwame to do his thing. "Playing a game with y'all is like watching squirrels run up a tree."

"Wow," Nadia and Wren scoffed at the same time.

"Go ahead Kwame, play your little game," Wren waved her brother along.

"You are a hater," Kwame laughed and wrapped his arms around Nadia's waist. "Alright, two truths and a lie...I ran over Wren's puppy...I am going in business for myself ... Nadia, I love you."

A pin could drop, and everyone could tell you where it was, due to how quiet everyone had gotten. Wren's mouth was on the floor, Brielle clasped her hands together and Nadia was trying to figure out the answer. "What did you say?"

Turning around to fully face him, Nadia studied Kwame's face to see if he really meant what he said. "I said I love you. With every fiber in my body, girl. I go to sleep so I can wake up to you. I frustrate the hell out of you just so I can make up with you and hold you in my arms. I purposely wait for you to get out the bed first, so I don't leave you laying there alone."

Nadia sat back on her knees and looked him with her brows pushed together. "What are you saying to me?"

Kwame chuckled and pulled Nadia closer to him. "I love you."

"Are you sure? Like you really love me?" Nadia still looked at him oddly, making Wren and Brielle flail their arms.

"Girl!" Brielle huffed. "Stop it. That man said he loved you. Say it back and kiss him."

24

2⁴
     Nadia Garrett

She bit her lip and stood up. Kwame looked up at her, unsure what she was going to do or say. "Could we talk about this inside?"

Clearing his throat, Kwame nodded his head and followed her inside. He knew that she was still guarded but he wasn't expecting her not to smile or acknowledge his confession. If the ring in his pocket was heavy before. It was heavier now that he was faced with the possibility that she wouldn't say it back or even want to get married.

Reaching the room, Nadia closed the door behind them and rested her back on the door. Silence fell between the awkward space between them. Kwame stood on the other side of the room and looked at her. "Why?"

"Why what?" he asked, not taking his eyes off of her.

"Why do you love me?" Nadia asked, chewing her lip. "I want to hear it."

Kwame inhaled and attempted to steady his nerves. "I have always loved you. That was just how it happened.

Since the day I laid my eyes on you, I knew. Shit just happened to go left, and it kept going left. I didn't want to step to you when I was still entertaining other women. I needed to make sure I was right for you, ready for you. I love your smart ass mouth. Your pieces and your pain. The way you can make something out of nothing. I love you."

Nadia locked the door and walked over to Kwame. Pulling him by the collar into her, she let her lips crash against his. Kwame placed his hands on her hips as Nadia fumbled with his belt buckle. She wasn't good with her feelings, but she could show him better than she could tell him.

In one swift action, Kwame picked her up off her feet and laid her on the bed. Removing his shirt, Nadia ran her hands down his abs and back to the top of his jeans. Completely undoing his belt and zipping his jeans, Nadia moaned against Kwame's lips as his hands yanked her leggings down her thighs.

It was a rush for her to become one with him; to feel his skin against hers and his breath on her skin. Naked and wrapped in his euphoria was everything she wanted right now. Once they were bare and surrounded by seductive aura, Kwame wrapped her legs around his waist. Pushing himself inside her, she moaned and held on to him.

Rotating her hips and riding his wave, her moans of pleasure rose in a crescendo. "Mmm, baby."

Nadia moved her hand from his back to his face, forcing him to look at her. "I love you, too."

Kwame's strokes were slow and purposeful. After kissing her lips, he placed her legs on his shoulders and continued to make her body overflow and tighten around him. Biting lightly on her calf, he grunted and leaned back down, pushing deeper inside. Nadia's eyes widened and her mouth made the shape of an O, but no sound came out. Her eyes rolled in the back of her head. He leaned down further so his mouth could hover over her ear.

"Marry me," he groaned. Those two words made her body flood more and began to pulse. He was ushering her into the warm rays of the sun. Like a flood of light, heat, and pleasure, the sound she was holding back escaped. "Marry me."

Kwame repeated himself, causing her to arch her back. "Say yes."

"Mmm, yesssss," she cried out in passion, gripping the sheets. "Yessss, oh yesss! Oh my God. YES!"

Sweat dripped from his brow while he pulled her orgasm out of her. Her legs shook against his chest. "Please don't stop."

He didn't. Not until he released, and she came again. Laying side-by-side they panted, attempting to catch their breath. Kwame reached for her hand and took it in his. "Did you hear me?"

Nadia squeezed her thighs closed as tight as she could, still on her wave of euphoria. She nodded her head and squeezed his hand. "I did."

Kwame reached over in the drawer of the nightstand and grabbed the ring box. Waiting until Nadia fully came down off her orgasm, Kwame sat up and walked around the bed to her side.

"Sit up, baby."

Slowly sitting up, Nadia looked over with eyes full of joy. "I love you and I don't wanna do this another day without calling you my wife and being your husband. Please do me the honor..."

"I was expecting something along the lines of, you're mine and that's it, now marry me," she giggled, holding her hand out. "I will marry you. I will fight you and love you. Now give me my ring, so I can thank you again."

Kwame laughed and opened the ring box and slid the ring on her finger. "You're so damn bossy."

"And now you get to have forevaaaaa. Get up here and kiss me."

Climbing back in the bed, he pulled her in her arms and kissed her. "I love you."

"Say it again."

"I love your mean ass."

"Good." Nadia's lips parted in a smile. "I love you, too. You broke me down like some kush."

She rolled her eyes and scoffed playfully, kissing him again. She never thought that she was would be so consumed and drenched in love. Nadia definitely didn't think that Kwame would be the man to provide her with the love and security her heart longed for.

"Well, I got one more thing for you," he chuckled, taking her hand in his and kissing her knuckles. "My company is disbanding, and I get all my clients. So, the business dealings that you and I have been doing with Izzy, is yours now."

"What? Why would you give that to me, you—"

"Shh. Because you've worked your ass off. I know how bad you want something of your own. So, it's all yours. When we get back, we can talk about that more." Pulling her on top of him, she straddled him and looked down at him.

"Thank you."

THE RESIDUE of her afterglow was still present all over her

face. Lifting her head off the pillow, she wiped the sleep from her eyes and rolled over to her back. Running her hand over her face, she felt the heavy ring Kwame blessed her with the night before. A smile crossed her face as she held her hand out and stared at the diamond dancing on her finger. Giddy was never a feeling she experienced but she was squealing, kicking and giggling underneath the sheets.

"I take it that you like it?" Kwame walked out of the bathroom and leaned on the wall with a smile on his face.

"You were not supposed to see that." She sat up and pushed her hands through her hair. "I really couldn't look at it last night, but baby in this light. You know I'm not flashy, but this is the shit."

Kwame laughed and walked over to her and kissed her face, "Come take a bath with me. I want to enjoy you a little more before Brielle and Wren steal you from me."

Standing up, she followed him into the bathroom. Resting in the tub with him laying between her thighs, she propped her head up in her hand and draped the other arm over his shoulder.

They enjoyed the intimacy and silence. Kwame's laid his head on her chest and listened to her heartbeat. He could sense that her mind was running a mile a minute. He made a mental note to talk about it when they got back home. He wanted to keep her in the moment and not worry about what was next. Picking up her hand off his chest, he kissed her palm and sat up and turned around. Kissing her neck, he brought her out her head and back to him.

After a quick love session in the bathtub, they washed off, got dressed and headed downstairs for breakfast.

Wren Daniels

· · ·

"THEY'RE ALIVE!" Roman shouted, seeing Kwame and Nadia walk into the open area from upstairs.

"Good!" Wren shouted from the kitchen. "Nadia come and make this French toast, I've tried three times."

"I told you to give to it up," Brielle replied. Nadia chuckled lightly and walked into the kitchen.

"How can you mess up French toast. Remember I told you to put heavy cream in the mix," she hummed, reaching over Brielle with her bedazzled hand. Nadia wasn't going to come out with the news, she was hoping that one of her nosey friends would catch on. "Caramel extract, cinnamon, heavy cream, and your eggs. It's going to be trash if you don't do it like that."

Wren hummed and moved to the fridge and pulled out the fruit. "Well, I'm happy you finally came out of hiding to save the day."

Taking over the mixing of a new batch of French toast, she smirked counting down the minute that one of them would grab her hand. "I do what I do best."

"Mmm," Brielle hummed. "Did you two talk about how you froze up after he told you he loved you?"

"I didn't freeze," Nadia defended. "It shocked the hell out of me for a second."

"You had to have known that he loved you," Wren chimed in. Nadia shrugged her shoulders.

"Part of me knew but hearing it is something different," she shared with her girls. "The other part of me was still waiting for the ball to drop."

"Nadia," Brielle spoke up after sniffing Wren's mimosa. "What's that?"

"What's what?" Nadia asked as if she was clueless about what Brielle was talking about and looking at.

"Hoe don't play with me." Brielle put Wren's glass down and grabbed Nadia's hand and gasped. "Wren...get over here."

"What's going on?" Wren asked, peeking over her shoulder after hurrying over from where she was standing. "Oh my God!"

Nadia smiled wide. Her smile was so big that her eyes disappeared behind her cheeks. "Are you serious?" Wren covered her mouth. "Y'all are getting married!"

"We are." Nadia's voice was so light and free as she looked over at their excitement.

Brielle wrapped Nadia up in her arms and Wren wrapped her arms around them. "You're really going to be my sister. Kwame!"

Taking off out the kitchen, Wren went to find her brother so she could hug him. "Why didn't you tell me you were going to propose! Who are you? Love and marriage? I am so proud of you."

Kwame hugged Wren and laughed. "I had to grow up. Couldn't chase ass all my damn life."

"But for a minute we were sure he was going to die with his dick in his hand," Julian scoffed in laughter and Roman rose his brow to look at him. "Shut up, Tiny Tim."

"Nigga, you opened the door. You thought I wasn't going to walk through it?" Roman asked as Julian shook his head.

"I am not that guy anymore," Julian chuckled. "I value my life."

"It comes a time where a boy has to grow into a man. We got to commit and do exactly what we say we're going to do. There was no way in hell that I was going to let her get away from me. I got years of bullshittin' to get right."

Wren smiled up at her brother and clasped her hands together. "You're going to be a great husband. There isn't anyone who can handle her like you."

"True shit," Julian spoke up.

"Because Lord knows," Roman laughed before dapping Kwame. "Proud of you bro. This is big shit."

"I know, married and old."

"For sure. But you owe me some bread. I said that you would be engaged by now." Roman held his hand out as Kwame pushed him away from him and laughed.

"Aht," Julian held his finger up and waved it in the air. "You said before we got here. You lost. That G is mine and I need it more. I got three kids."

"You run an ER, quit frontin'," Roman laughed. "I'm going to close my eyes and you're going to have five kids."

"The hell he is!" Brielle shouted from the kitchen and walking out with food. "Don't be making plans with my uterus. I'm tired."

2 5

Kwame Franklin

Two weeks had passed since Nadia agreed to marry him. Underneath the smile she wore, he could sense there was a bit of hesitation about moving forward. He wanted to ask her, but he didn't want to hear that she wasn't ready. Instead, he was trying to string the pieces together correctly so he could address her fear.

Easing into the house, he heard low voices from the living room. It was Thursday night and Nadia, Brielle, and Wren were enjoying a girls' night in. He normally tried working later on their girl nights so she could have her time. Typically, by the time he got home they were gone. But from the tone of the conversation, they were in the middle of deep conversation. Placing his keys down silently, he inched closer to the living room and listened to Nadia's voice cry.

"I don't want him to think that I don't want to marry him. Or that I'm not happy. I am," she sniffled. "I have never been so happy. But when I think about my wedding, my dad isn't there. My mother isn't there. I'm not saying that you guys aren't enough. But in the traditional sense of how this is supposed to go, I will never have my dad give me away. That fucks with me."

"Nadia, I know he will understand that. It's not like he doesn't know that you miss your father and your relationship with your mother isn't there. You got to talk to him. You aren't alone anymore, stop internalizing stuff thinking it's too much for someone else to carry. I have never seen my brother so happy and so complete. He wants to carry your pieces so he can put them back together. Let him do it," Wren soothed her. "Please, not for him or us. But for you. Please."

"You got to talk to your man. Y'all are about to make a commitment for life. Honestly, doesn't matter if we're there or not. It's about you two. At the end of the day, that's the only thing that matters," Brielle spoke up. "Okay?"

Kwame stepped back and pulled his phone out his pocket and walked outside. Dialing Isabella's number, he pressed the phone to his ear and waited for her to pick up. "Hey, Kwame. What's going on?"

"I need you to do me a huge favor and I need you to keep this under wraps," he spoke up, looking over his shoulder.

"Anything. What's up?"

"How fast can you set up a trip to Catalina for me. Same villa and everything. I need an officiant and dinner. I can figure everything else out," he shared, rubbing his hands over his low cut.

"If you give me a week, I can have everything good to go," she smiled through the phone.

"I owe you one."

"No, you don't. Just keep her happy is all I ask. You two have done more than enough for me," she assured him. "I'll get everything together. I'll call when everything is good to go."

"Thank you."

The front door opened, and Kwame turned around to see Wren and Brielle saying their goodnights. "Y'all be safe," Nadia waved before looking up at Kwame with her puffy eyes.

"We will. Hey Kwame, bye Kwame," Wren and Brielle waved, walking past him.

Kwame looked down at Nadia and sighed. "You good?"

"Can I talk to you?" she asked in a low voice.

"Of course," he nodded, walking into the house behind her. Securing the front door, he followed her into the kitchen and watched as she fixed him a plate of food. "What's going on with you? You've been quiet."

Just because he knew what was wrong didn't mean that he didn't want to hear it from her. Nadia put his plate in front of him and sucked on her bottom lip for a minute before leaning on the counter. "I don't want you to think that I am not happy. Because I am. I got in my head and started thinking about our wedding. All I saw was your family and, on my side there wasn't anyone and it upset me. All I have is you and the crew. That's it. I didn't want my wedding to be like that and I damn sure don't want to upset you or be upset because of that."

Kwame nodded his head and took a bite of his food.

"You got to understand this. I don't care who's there. I'm not marrying them. I'm marrying you. That's all the matters to me. Tell me what's going on in your head, please."

Nadia sighed and nodded her head and stood up. She wiped her face and exhaled again as Kwame's phone chimed.

Damn, she did that fast. He said to himself as she read over the text from Isabella. The villa is available in a month, it's yours.

Shooting her a quick text back thanking her, he locked his phone and reached out to Nadia. "It's going to be okay. Think about what you want and tell me, I'll make it shake."

Resting her head on his shoulder and kissing his cheek, she rubbed his back silently thanking him. "Put your plate in the dishwasher, I'm going upstairs."

He was going to give her the rest of the night to deal with her feelings. But tomorrow they were going to move forward.

Nadia Garrett

NADIA WRAPPED Kamaiyah in her arms and hugged her tightly. It was official; she was a high school graduate and didn't have to do any alternative schooling because of her pregnancy. For the day, they all gathered at Julian and Brielle's to celebrate. Roman finally broke down and gifted her a car to get back and forth from work. He wasn't ready to let her out his sight just yet, but evidentially Kamaiyah would be on her own using the tools that they all had given her to flourish.

"I am so proud of you," Nadia hummed into Kamaiyah's

ear. Out of everyone, their relationship was tight. Nadia had taken Kamaiyah under her wing and adopted her as her little sister.

"You're going to make me cry," Kamaiyah whined, stepping back and holding Nadia's hand. "Thank you for everything. Seriously."

"I told you I had you. I will always have you. Okay?"

Kamaiyah nodded her head and hugged her one last time before Kwame opened the car door for Nadia. "I love you. I'll see you later."

"Love you too!" Nadia blew her a kiss and climbed into the car. Settling into her seat, she buckled her seat belt and put her feet up on the dashboard. Kwame finished joking with Julian and Roman, who stood on the porch shouting something at him. Nadia wasn't paying much attention to it. After the emotional day of watching Kamaiyah graduate, she just wanted to get home and binge watch whatever she could find on Netflix.

Kwame climbed into the running car, put it in drive and took her hand in his. "You look tired."

"I'm exhausted. All these displays of emotion are draining me," she mumbled with her eyes closed. "I think y'all are trying to kill me."

Kwame laughed and pulled out Julian's driveway and headed back to her house. "Babe. Really?"

"Really, I'm so in tune with my feelings. I hate that shit," she smirked. "Y'all are turning me into a ball of mush. I am a hard ass bitch from Oakland. I don't do emotions."

"You also didn't do commitment, or any involvement with a man longer than a night before you snuck out and forgot his name," Kwame chuckled at Nadia's old tendencies. "You were hell."

"Don't count me out yet, baby. I still got it," she joked,

cracking an eye open to see him looking at her like she lost her mind.

"Girl, don't you even try me," he warned with a scoff. "You still got it. Yeah, okay...Play with me if you want to."

"You are so dramatic," Nadia laughed and looked at him.

Kwame kissed his teeth and rolled his eyes. "Nah, you be testing limits and trying to see what you can get away with. You and your man ass ways will get your ass in some trouble you can't get out of."

"You know I like trouble," she smiled wide.

"Mhmm," Kwame rose his brow. "You don't like walking and talking I see."

"Oh relax, no one talks to me. They see this big ass ring and turn around."

Kwame pulled up to the stop light and started clapping his hands. "That's exactly why I dropped all the bread on it. I'm not playing with these niggas. You're mine and that's it."

"That's it huh?"

"That's it. I earned my right to talk my shit," he finalized. Nadia pressed her lips together. "Say I didn't."

"Oh baby, you earned the right to talk all the shit you want. But do not forget that I earned the right to talk my shit, too."

"You can't let me have the last word huh?"

"Never."

Pulling up the house, Kwame put the car in park and killed the engine. She was complaining about being in her feelings all day, but she was going to be in her feelings for the rest of the weekend. Walking into the house behind her, Nadia walked up the stairs into the bedroom to a galore of fresh cut flowers. "Aw, baby."

"You like them?" he walked into the closet and pulled their suitcases out.

"I do. But tonight, you might get lazy side booty I'm tired," she shared before looking at him walk out the closet with suitcases and two garment bags. "What are you doing?"

"We are going to Catalina in the morning," he announced. Nadia rose her brow and looked at him suspiciously. "Don't say anything about work. I know we're about to be busy, but I need one weekend with you before our schedules get crazy."

"Okay..." she agreed, looking at him from the corner of her eyes. "You packed my stuff?"

"I did."

"I need to make sure you got everything."

"No, you don't," he chuckled. "Got it. I'm going to put this in the car."

"What are you up to?" she questioned, watching him walk out the room with their things. "Kwame..."

"I can't hear you!"

"I swear," she groaned before smiling and going to take a shower.

26

2⁶

Nadia Garrett

WALKING INTO THE VILLA, she laughed. "The same villa? Really?"

"I had to redo that weekend. Change your association with Catalina," he shared, bringing their bags in. He watched as she walked through the villa and out to the balcony. Looking down on the beach, she spotted a few people set up for a wedding.

"Oh look, someone's getting married," she smiled, surveying the beach. Feeling Kwame's arms wrap around her waist and his lips caress her shoulders, she relaxed in his embrace.

"I know," he hummed against her skin. "We are."

Nadia broke away from him and turned around. "Say what?"

"That's our wedding set up. Just me and you. No stress, no expectations from anyone, just all this love."

She had no words. She stared at him as her eyes flooded with tears threatening to spill over. "How did you do all of this?"

"I called in some favors and snooped around your planning books. Looked at all the shit you circled and put it together and here we are," Kwame looked down at the love of his life and wiped her tears. "I love you, Nadia Garrett and I don't want to spend not another day without you being my wife."

"Kwame Franklin," she released his name and placed her hands on his chest. "You are something else."

"Oh, baby. This is just the tip," he chuckled, hearing a knock at the door. "That's the photographer, your makeup artist, and your hair stylist. I'll see you in a few hours."

"What am I wearing?" Nadia smirked, unable to let go of the idea that he had put everything together.

"It's hanging up. Go ahead." Stepping out her way so she could get ready. Before she reached the door, she turned around to flash one final smile at him before she met him at the altar.

HER NERVES WERE in shambles as she stood in front of the full-length mirror and looked over her silky straight hair, perfect nude makeup and two-piece gown. The high waisted skirt with the split up the thigh, fell over her hips perfectly. The cropped tank exposed just enough skin of her mid-section. The only person who knew about this gown was Isabella.

She made a mental note to thank her for making sure this came together perfectly. Flattening a flyaway, Nadia looked back over at the glam squad and thanked them for making her vision come true. The photographer didn't miss a moment of her getting ready or Kwame waiting nervously for her to walk down.

"Everything is ready," the photographer announced. "You ready? You look so beautiful."

"Thank you," Nadia inhaled to keep from crying and ruining her makeup. Picking up the bottom of her skirt she walked out the room to see Brielle and Wren in their dresses, waiting on her to walk out. "Oh my God."

Nadia covered her mouth as the tears she was fighting to keep back escaped. "Stop it. I can't take it."

The girls laughed and hugged her. "You think that he was going to let you get married without us. Stop crying you're going to ruin your make up."

Nadia dropped down to a squat as she cried in her hands. After a few moments, she stood up and sighed. "I am so happy."

"You are so beautiful," Brielle cooed, wiping her face. "You have been there for us through everything. Even when we did dumb shit. We were never going to let you go through the most important day of your life without supporting you."

"I can't believe y'all didn't give me a heads up," Nadia smacked her lips while the makeup artist retouched her face.

"How do you think that dress fit? Kwame is capable of a lot, but some things need a woman's touch," Wren laughed, handing Nadia her bouquet. "You're getting married girl."

"My heart is so full," Nadia admitted. "I don't ever want to forget this feeling."

"Ah, the woman who doesn't do emotion is loving it right about now, huh?" Brielle laughed. "Let's get you married."

Picking up the bottom of her dress, Brielle and Wren escorted Nadia down to the beach where Kwame, Julian, and Roman stood barefoot in gray dress pants and crisp white shirts. Their top button was unbuttoned, and their sleeves were rolled up.

Kwame looked down the aisle at Nadia and winked at her before licking his lips. He wasn't a crier but watching her smile as brightly as she did as she marched towards him to the music, he felt his chest swell.

"I must have rehearsed my lines, a thousand times until I had them memorized. Bet when I get up the nerve to tell you, the words never seem to come out right," Patti LaBelle's classic sung by Keke Wyatt through the speakers. "If only you knew how much I do, do love you. Oh, if only if you knew, how much I do, do need you."

Wiping her tears and rubbing her lips against one another as she walked toward Kwame. She couldn't have been happier. She couldn't have been prouder of herself, of him. She allowed herself to feel something other than fear and pain. Letting her guard down just an inch for him to break in and steal her heart and replacing it with his. The man she pushed away, fought with, treated like shit was the man that covered her without question. He was always in her corner, for that she would spend the rest of her life trying to repay that debt.

Standing at the altar and holding his hand in hers, she watched as the tears fell down his cheeks as the officiant spoke. Julian placed his hand on his shoulder and squeezed it lightly. Nadia forgot about the fact that her father wasn't there to give her away. She forgot that her mother hadn't been a mother to her. She forgot about everyone and everything that hurt her. Everything that broke her heart prior to this point was null and void. They didn't matter anymore. She was standing with the only person that made her heart burst with love. She was surrounded by the people who loved her more than her own family ever could.

This was her family; this was her happy ending. As Kwame and Nadia exchanged vows, their wedding party closed in around them and reinforced their promise. Nadia and Kwame had forced them all to be the best versions of their selves and they were going to reinforce Nadia and Kwame's every day.

They rode together, they cried together, they went through the worst storms and always came out on the other end together. That was the fight for love. That was the earth-shattering, mountain moving, stargazing love that they deserved.

After being named Mr. and Mrs. Kwame Nasir Franklin, they retreated down the aisle hand-in-hand.

Sitting at the long table set up on the balcony, Isabella made everything that the couple loved. "I got something to say," Roman spoke up, standing to his feet.

"Oh, shit," Julian mumbled, rolling his eyes. "Stand on a phone book so we can see you!"

"Boy, I'll knock your teeth out your head," Roman shot back.

"Where is the love?" Julian teased. "I'm sorry I haven't hugged you today."

"No, you haven't, and I feel a way about that," Roman admitted. Julian pushed his seat out and stood up to walk around that table and hug Roman. "I love you man."

"I love you too man!"

Brielle and Wren rolled their eyes and laughed. "They are ridiculous."

"Okay, I feel better now," Roman laughed before looking down the table at Nadia and Kwame. "I want to just toast you two. For fighting like hell to get here. Y'all deserve everything good. Everything. You two have been our best friends, our lifelines and our support system. You never faltered or left us hanging. Y'all have pulled up and made that shit work. I pray that every day is better than the day before and that you never forget that everything you need is right by your side."

Kwame held his glass up and nodded his head in Roman's direction. Julian picked up his glass and smiled. "I remember when Brielle and I were going through the worst time of our lives and Kwame told me that if I loved my wife the way I said I did, I would do whatever I had to do to get her back. Bro, that shit saved my life." Julian paused and hummed and let his tears drop out his eyes. "You have always been my brother. You rode with me, you spoke life into me, and to see you stepping into your kingdom is big shit and I am happy as hell that you finally locked your queen down. I love y'all."

Nadia smiled and wiped the tears from Kwame's cheeks. "I swear I'm no bitch, but y'all niggas breaking me down."

Wren stood up by Roman and wiped her tears and exhaled. "I am so happy I got to witness this. This is a testament that the love that is for you, will work through all of our hurt and broken pieces to heal and rebirth us. To see my best friend and my brother so happy in love and leaning on each other and forgetting all of the other shit it took to get to this point, it's beautiful. I want the best of life to fall on you two. All the love, all the happiness, all the wealth, and all the babies. Y'all deserve that. Remain true to who you are and love like the world is ending."

"I can't take no more of this," Nadia whined, patting her face with the cloth napkin. "Y'all are breaking me down."

"Too bad because they saved the best for last," Brielle popped up and locked eyes with Nadia. "You are that bitch. You are a queen. You are powerful. You are love. Everything you denied yourself of, you possessed it the entire time. I am so proud that you let Kwame work your nerves to no end and apply that pressure to turn you into a diamond. I am so proud to say that you are my corner. Nothing is going to stop y'all as long as you hold on to each. Nothing is going to break you as long as you communicate. Y'all are Bonnie and Clyde ride or die don't ever lose what it is that makes y'all, y'all."

"We love y'all so much," their friends shouted and clapped their hands. After hugs and a round of shots, they danced until the sun went down.

Kwame rocked Nadia in his arms slowly as he kissed her face. "Mrs. Franklin."

"Mr. Franklin."

"I love you."

"I love you." Nadia locked her hands around his waist. "You know what I want?"

"More cake?"

"Mm mm," she hummed, biting her bottom lip. "I want you. All of you, forever."

Kwame lifted his head to see their friends caught up with one another. "Let me start right now."

Leading her into the villa and to the bedroom, he kicked the door shut and picked her up to lay her down on the bed. He kissed every inch of her skin; he took his time. He wanted to make love to her; hold her close while she cheered his name. Moan his worship into the nook her neck.

Their bodies were one, their eyes were hood, they were drenched and covered in love. It filled the room, it peeked through the blinds and illuminated that fusing skin.

Kwame pushed himself inside of her walls as deep as he could, and Nadia gladly welcomed him. "I love you," she moaned, digging into his flesh as the sweat allowed his body to glide over hers so effortlessly. "So much."

"Mm," Kwame moaned, no longer caring if he lost himself in her. She had him now and there was no turning back. Nadia giggled and pushed him up. She had him where she wanted him, on the edge. She as going to take all of him, every drop.

Dropping to his back, he watched as Nadia straddled him and took him in with a smile on her face. Rocking her hips against his, she leaned down and kissed his chest, biting it lightly after every peck. She rotated her hips up and down on his pole. Gripping, dripping, pulsating, ass smacking, groans, and crescendos of I love yous, until he exploded inside of her and she covered him with all that she had. They spilled over.

Nadia laid on his chest and kissed his jawline. "Tagged and bagged."

He laughed and put his hands in her hair. "What's that?"

"Tracks." Nadia shrugged her shoulders.

"I want you, naked baby. No makeup, no extra's just you."

"Well, it's sewed in, so if you want it out, you're to have to help."

Kwame sat up, "Alright. Where're the scissors?"

He loved putting his hands in her hair, for him she

didn't need anything to enhance her beauty. She was perfect the way she was.

Nadia got out the bed and get through her bag for a pair of scissors. Returning back to the bed, she sat down on the floor between his legs. "If you cut my hair, I will fight you."

"You know I fight back; I'm dying to break your back in," Kwame chuckled. "I'm not going to cut your hair, girl. I love it too much."

"Alright. Stop talking and focus."

"I can multitask."

Nadia laughed and rolled her eyes and sighed. "You've blown my mind."

"I wanted you to have everything that was important surrounding you," he hummed, removing the tracks from her hair.

Nadia smile would probably never fade. The imprint he left on her soul would be carried with her everywhere she went for the rest of her days.

After taking hair out and unbraiding her hair, she stood naked between Kwame's legs while he shook his hands through her hair. "There she is. That's my wife."

Cradling his face in her hands, she giggled and passionately kissed his lips. "Thank you."

"Always."

Nadia Franklin

THREE MONTHS HAD PASSED since Kwame and Nadia tied the knot. It was full of passionate lovemaking, laughs, inside jokes and occasional attitude that never lasted longer than an hour. For two weeks, they'd been closing on their forever home and making sure the homes they owned while they were single were ready to be sold.

They welcomed the break from packing and moving to celebrate with Julian and Brielle. Wren decided to host a gender reveal party for them. Since they missed this moment the first time around, it was important that they had it now.

Julian was rooting for team girl just as hard as Brielle was pulling for a boy. Their friends stood back and waited for them to shoot their smoke cannons in the air. "Five, four, three, two, one!" Everyone counted down before an explosion of pink smoke and confetti filled the space surrounding them.

Screams and cheers filled the air. Nadia ran over to Brielle and wrapped her up in her arms. "We got a girl!"

The guys congratulated Julian by handing him a glass of Hennessy. "I am so happy that's over. Now. I can eat."

Nadia laughed as Brielle dropped down into a chair and rubbed her belly. "I'll go get you some food."

Wren followed Nadia into the house to grab the food and bring it out. "I need to get Roman out of here before he gets any ideas."

Nadia laughed and shook her head. "Give that man a baby."

"Not yet, I like all of my attention," Wren laughed. "But you can have one for me."

"What makes you think I don't like my attention?" Nadia asked. "I love rolling over in the middle of the night and getting it in without worrying about waking up a baby."

Wren shook her head and walked into the kitchen to see Keera sitting at the table. "Ah hell. Who let the trash in?"

"Don't act like y'all didn't think I was going to pop back up," Keera chuckled and stood up. "I was hoping I would see Brielle trying to compete with me instead of you two."

Nadia looked over Wren's shoulder and saw Keera. It was the perfect time for Nadia to finish what she started. Pushing Wren out the way, she didn't bother replying to her. Instead, Keera's face was met by Nadia's open palm. Watching her stumble backward, Nadia tagged her face over and over, Wren jumped in and started helping Nadia whip her ass.

They were going to beat her until she couldn't lift her head up. And then they would drag get out with the trash.

Nadia picked up Keera by the collar and started dragging her to the door.

Kwame was walking in the back door to find out what was taking the two of them so long to bring the food out. "What are you doing!"

Catching his wife with her hands around Keera's throat and headed to the door, he growled lowly. "Roman, come here!"

Wren groaned, knowing that Roman was not with the shits when it came down to her catching a charge or two. Roman walked in after Kwame called him and pointed at Nadia and Wren trying to get rid of Keera. Roman huffed and pulled Wren away from Keera. "It only takes one of y'all to beat her ass. Not two."

Kwame attempted to get Nadia to let loose of Keera, but she pushed him away and grabbed Keera by the back of her neck and pushed her out the house. "Don't you bring your bum ass back around her."

Keera was hard of hearing but that ass whopping spoke louder than any amount of yelling. She was lost and disoriented as she climbed into her car. The look Nadia shot both Roman and Kwame warned them about helping her.

Feeling queasy, Nadia pushed by Kwame and ran into the bathroom and closed the door behind her. "What the hell just happened?" Roman asked Kwame.

"I'll be back. Can you take the food out? And Wren don't even bring this up okay?"

Wren smiled in satisfaction and nodded her head. "No problem at all."

"Wren, I swear you like taking felony chances," Roman groaned, walking behind her into the kitchen and looking at the mess they made.

"No, I don't but I take the chance to beat her ass over

and over." Roman rolled his eyes and her comment and started cleaning up the kitchen. He looked at her and smiled.

"Proud of you though."

"I know you are."

Kwame walked into the half-bath to see Nadia's head hung over the toilet as she threw up everything she ate. His heart dropped and exploded with happiness. Grabbing her hair, he stood by silently while she continued to throw up.

Once it passed, he got her a warm towel and wiped her face. Flushing the toilet and putting the lid down and Nadia sat down and sighed. "Well, there's the proof I was looking for."

"You're pregnant?" he squinted with a smile. Nadia's head nodded slowly. "How far along?"

"I don't know. I know that I've been dealing with this for the last week. I was going to take a test before I told you. I'm been cramping bad and feeling sick, so I knew," she shared, looking up at her husband.

"And you were out there fighting like you lost your damn mind? What the hell is wrong with you?" Kwame palmed his face, trying to calm down. "Baby, you can't be doing that shit."

"I know," Nadia groaned and dropped her head in her hands.

Kwame was trying to read her. "Are you not happy?"

"I'm scared," she revealed. "I'm so scared."

"Hey," he spoke up and lifted her head up. "We're riding. We're going to be parents."

His smile was enormous. "I've been waiting on you to say something. I purposely tried to knock you up in Catalina. I'm actually surprised it didn't happen sooner. I'm

Terry's son, I've been trying to impregnate your ass since Scottsdale."

"You get on my damn nerves," Nadia chuckled as Kwame pulled her to her feet.

"I know and I love you."

"Good because now you're really stuck with me. Can we eat...I'm hungry again."

Rejoining the group, Kwame sat by his wife with a smile on his face. Brielle had no idea that both Wren and Nadia had taken out her trash once and for all. Even though he was highly upset that Nadia had taken it upon herself to fight, he knew how she was. He would never be able to change the fact that she was going to protect everything she loved at all times, no matter the costs. He was going to have to pray that the bundle of joy they were expecting was going to slow her down a bit.

He was just overjoyed to have his wife and his family. He watched as everyone was content about where they were in life. The only way to go from here was up. There wouldn't be a day that passed where we didn't gladly play to win the game of love, step in the ring and go round-for-round or fight for everything he wanted and everything he believed in.

He was complete. They all were. Life has taught them a valuable lesson about love.

Without it you were nothing.

The End

FIGHT FOR LOVE

Love me deep, stroke me slow
Take your time, to the top we go
Love me long, love my strong
Feed until I'm full
When I fight, I'll need your energy
That perfect synergy to forever
Fight for you
Fight for us
Fight for love

-A.P.

AFTERWORD

Thank you so much for reading this piece of art. I saved their story for last because it required careful creation of their love story. It has made my heart full to set out on this journey and see through with Love, The Series. I am so thankful for the amazing support during this creative process. Jessi, thank you. Dominique, thank you. Sidni, thank you. I love you all to the moon and back and I am so honored to have dope women like you in my corner and pushing me to be better and do better.

Brielle, Nadia, and Wren were all pieces of women that I know and that I love. Thank you for entrusting me to tell your stories.

Until next time. Live, love, grow. And remember to run your marathon until God calls you home.

TMC.

- A.P.

ALSO BY AUBREÉ PYNN

Thank you for reading! Make sure you check out my catalog:

Dope Boys I&II

Everything is Love

Mistletoe Meltdown

My Love for You

My Love for You, Always

Say He'll Be My Valentine

The Way You Lie

The Way You Lie: The Aftershock

Run from Me

Love Over All

The Game of Love

Love Knockout

Connect with me on my social media:

IG: @aubreepynn

TWITTER: @aubreepynn

Facebook: Aubreé Pynn

Check out my website:

Aubreepynnwrites.wordpress.com

A million words, in a million books, is never thank you enough for your support.

Made in the
USA
Middletown, DE